The Vag

Frank Bonham

The Vagabundos

THE VAGABUNDOS

by Frank Bonham

E. P. DUTTON & CO., INC.   NEW YORK

To Gloria with love

chapter **1**

Around bedtime on that strange night, Eric's father came into the family room wearing old trousers and a sweatshirt and smacking a flashlight into his palm. For a moment he watched Eric, who was crouched beside the pool table searching through a jumble of colored balls for an easy shot. Eric could feel energy radiating from him like sparks.

"How about a run, Champ?" said Mr. Hansen heartily. "Gotta work off a little steam before bed. Thought I'd jog down to the reservoir. Hup! hup!" he added.

"I'd better not," Eric said. "I did a mile after school. I'd be bushed tomorrow."

Mr. Hansen scoffed. "What's a mile to a two-mile champion? Come on, it's a great night! The moon's out and there's no traffic."

Eric glanced at the television set. He had turned the sound off during a commercial; a huckster with a jar of iron pills was still wheedling, cajoling, and threatening. Eric squinted down the cue, sawed it back and forth, and made his shot. On the green cloth, the bright constellation of pool balls regrouped itself like the particles of an atom. A ball dropped—the cue ball.

His father prodded him playfully with the flashlight. "See, you're all tensed up! Better go with me. Jogging's a great tonic for the nerves."

Hup, hup, Eric said to himself. "Can't," he said, drifting back to the television set.

"The way you've been training lately," his father needled him, "that Oceanside High kid will run the pants off you Saturday. *Vámonos!*"

A big, rangy man with red hair touched with gray on the temples, long-limbed and florid, a Viking with a small paunch, Mr. Hansen did a few running-in-place steps. Eric gave a pained smile. His father had recently picked up this habit of inflating himself with enthusiasm the way you would pump up a tire. It was embarrassing, and unless Eric matched this artificial animation, his ardor quickly cooled. Apparently it took two to teeter-totter.

"I can't!" Eric repeated. "I'm going to bed as soon as this is over. I'm tired."

"Got your homework done?" Severity was now beginning to sharpen his father's voice. Eric sensed, with apprehension, that his mood had definitely started a swing. Turning up the sound, he sat down.

"Yeah, it's done," he said.

"You're not sore, are you?" asked his father.

"What about?"

"You know what about."

"No, I don't." Eric kept his eyes on the tube, aware of his father planting his hands on his hips and glaring at him.

"Because I wouldn't put the motorcycle back together for you."

"Heck, I only tore it down Sunday!" Eric was baffled.

"And this is Tuesday, and it's still lying all over the garage floor."

"Okay, okay! So it's lying on the floor," said Eric, in exasperation. "I'll fix it. No sweat."

Abruptly his father reached out and cut the television set off cold. His thin-skinned features were red with anger. Eric stared at him.

"What's the idea?" he demanded.

"I'm talking to you, that's what the idea is!"

Eric struck his brow. "I *told* you, Dad! I've got a *test*—"

"I'm not talking about that! I'm talking about the motorcycle! When I bought it for you, the deal was that you'd do your own mechanical work. The only thing you're going to get out of that death trap beside fractures is an appreciation of fine machinery. And now—"

Eric groaned, feeling as though he had been trapped into the argument. What were they talking about? Homework, running, or his motorcycle? He said, with passion,

"I appreciate it, I appreciate it! I'll have it running this weekend." He shook his head in despair, then added, "I thought you were going for a run."

"Don't get smart," his father snapped. "You know I'll get sick of seeing it scattered around and fix it myself, as I always do." He raised one finger. "Okay! But if it isn't running by Sunday, I'm going to sell it."

"Fine!" Eric retorted. They confronted each other. With nothing really settled, however, Mr. Hansen seemed unable to think of anything else to argue about, and they merely stared. Eric's gaze wandered. He muttered,

"I'm sorry I can't run with you. But I'm already tired."

His father forced a grin. "Think nothing of it. Not the first time I've run alone."

He tossed the flashlight, caught it, switched the television set on again and left the room. Eric heard the front door bang.

In a few minutes he turned the set off. He felt an itch of guilt, though he could see no reason why he should have run. After leaving the family room, he got a cold apple from the refrigerator and started upstairs to his bedroom.

He wondered why, when he was younger, Life With Father had been a ball, whereas now they were constantly sniping at each other. Probably, like most of the men around here, what his father needed was a job. Most of the men he knew were continually knocking themselves out trying to keep busy. Yet when you already had it made financially, it seemed foolish to take a nine-to-five job. All Eric knew for sure was that things had been a lot more satisfactory before his father sold the Han-DeeRench tool plant and retired. He took a large bite of apple, so cold it made his front teeth ache. Mabel, the owner-manager of the Village Coffee Shop, called the retired executives of Rancho Sereno, Mothball Admirals. That really nailed it down, he thought. Admirals of the Mothball Fleet, standing on the bridges of warships that would never cruise again. And the sad truth, he feared, was that his father was right up there in dress blues with the others.

In his room, he stripped to his shorts and brushed his teeth. Making a monkey-grin at himself, he inspected the upper tooth he had chipped a month ago when he flipped on the motorcycle. He liked the ruggedness it imparted to his somewhat simple features—smallish blue eyes, rope-colored hair, and bleached eyebrows.

He scowled, then quirked one eyebrow and grinned raffishly. With disdain, however, he still saw the face of Joe Average. He had an odd feeling about himself. That the body of Eric Hansen was inhabited by a soft, submissive creature like a hamster; but inside the hamster there lived yet another animal, the Secret Boss of Eric Hansen, brash and self-confident, an animal which unfortunately could seldom be heard by people on the outside. If it ever took over, there would be some changes made, he vowed. But in the meantime, while he waited, his deportment resembled that of a stagehand accidentally shoved onto the stage, who had to fake a few lines before he could slink off.

After switching off the bedroom light, he stood at the window. The deep-walled old mansion was silent except for the creaking of its bones. It was California Moorish, built in an era when contractors had to know elementary Spanish to follow the blueprints. His sister Debbie, fourteen, was long since in bed; his mother had not returned from a Trails Committee meeting of the Riding Club. With poor grace, he did a few leg exercises. Coach Martin had been after him lately for not training the way he had last year. His time for the two-mile run was slipping. But he still held the record for Sorrento High.

Well, man, if you want the truth, Eric was tempted to tell the coach, it's not much fun loping around the track all night with your tongue hanging out, for a crowd that's cheering pole vaulters and sprinters.

Below him, the landscape was emerging in cold photographic tones. The house rested on a hilltop. The driveway curved down through the Hansens' lemon grove to a winding blacktop road. Across the road lay a long, silvered pasture enclosed by dark groves of orange and avocado trees with a tiny lake beyond. In the middle of a rise-on-toes, Eric stiffened like a hunting dog.

A light gleamed on the west shore of the lake. A new house was being built over there; the light seemed to be inside it. Vandals? He scurried to the closet, pawed through some paraphernalia on a shelf, and darted back with a pair of binoculars. The light flitted aimlessly through the house, finally coming to rest in one place like a lightning bug.

Could his father be prowling the house? he wondered. He haunted every new home that was built, a sort of unofficial contractor. As soon as the framing went up, he was right there with a list of suggestions for the builder.

Don't forget the fireblocks between those joists, fella! It'll never pass inspection that way. You should have put your kitchen wiring in the slab, too. With all those windows, there's no place for wall wiring.

Eric recalled, in fact, his returning from the new house one day last week complaining about the way the fireplace was being constructed. "There's a thin column of bricks on one side that'll crack the first time it gets hot," he had said. "And for design, that fireplace will take the *Mad* Magazine perpetual trophy."

Had he dropped in tonight to shake his head over it some more? Actually, Eric did not think he could have run that far in so short a time.

Maybe, he reflected, he should call Sergeant Harris, the one-man police force of Rancho Sereno. Old Sarge, however, would not appreciate being dragged out in the middle of the night on a false alarm. Eric twisted the eyepieces of the binoculars. The light seemed to have settled permanently in that one room. Hmmm. Vandals would be all over the place, he thought, and would probably work without a light.

What it probably was, he decided finally, was the owner of the house, Mr. Cresswell, checking on how many nails the carpenters had bent that day. According to Mabel, he was so tight that he got three estimates before investing in an evening paper.

Eric laid aside the binoculars. He did a few more exercises, pulled on his pajama pants, and crawled into bed.

He was awakened by the crunch of tires in gravel. He punched the pillow, thinking, Mom's home. But on hearing men's voices, he raised his head. One of the voices was definitely his father's. He could not identify the other, but it sounded familiar.

Foggy with sleep, he padded to the window.

". . . I don't have any choice, Mr. Hansen," said the second man. "I have to make a report. It's as simple as that."

"The only thing that's simple, dammit, is you!" Eric's father retorted. And now Eric could see the outline of the dome light atop Sergeant Harris's police car. "If you keep your mouth shut, they won't notice a damned thing!"

"You're not doing yourself any good with an attitude like this, Mr. Hansen," said the sergeant. "I won't charge you unless Cresswell gets steamed up. Technically, it's vandalism, though. You may have to pay to put things back the way they were."

"In a pig's eye!" said Mr. Hansen. He strode to the house. The police car rolled away.

Eric hurried back to bed. Judas Priest, it *had* been his father in the new house! *Vandalism!* What had he done? Put *what* things back the way they were? The fireplace?

Lying motionless, he listened to a door bang and feet ascending the stairs. A moment later he heard his mother's car arrive. His father seemed almost to run up the stairs, past Eric's room to his own. The door closed.

When Mrs. Hansen came in, all was quiet. Whatever had happened in the dark house across the lake, Eric's father was keeping it to himself.

chapter **2**

At seven-ten, woozy from lack of sleep, Eric slouched to a rear seat of the school bus. He took a place on the side next to the new house, and as the bus passed it he stared intently at the long, low structure. Workmen in white coveralls were already shambling around mixing plaster and carrying boards. Eric looked for signs of vandalism, but saw none. But of course he could not see the fireplace.

Some deal, he thought, having to worry about your parents' behavior! My father, the vandal.

Now and then the bus stopped and picked up a few young-sters. By the time it had zigzagged its way across the Ranch, as local people called Rancho Sereno, it was filled with boys. Only a half-dozen girls rode the bus to the Union High School in Sorrento Beach. Most of them were hauled off by car pool to Miss Pridmore's School in nearby La Jolla. At Miss Pridmore's, wearing somewhat dowdy Black Watch skirts and jackets and starched blouses, they were kept on ice until time for college.

No one had ever explained the system to Eric, but he figured it out this way. Parents thought that boys might profit from exposure to poorer kids whose fathers worked in plants in San Diego or at the manual trades. Apparently girls did not need this kind of toughening, so they were hothoused alone in private schools.

Eric did not fully come to life until biology. Then suddenly he remembered. It was Careers Day! A scientist from Scripps Institution of Oceanography was going to talk to them about oceanography as a career. Eric had even bought a new notebook days ago, and labeled it: *Oceanography.*

He had been interested in the sea for years. He had once kept a salt-water aquarium, stocking it with specimens he took while skin-diving. A few months ago, following brief flirtations with a half-dozen other majors, he had settled on oceanography as a career. An evening of skin-diving movies and visits to Sea World had actually pushed him into the decision.

Full of anticipation, he hurried into class and took his seat. With his special notebook open, he studied the large, rather disheveled stranger sitting beside Mr. Brown, the teacher. On the blackboard Mr. Brown had written:

Dr. Crabtree.

Eric felt a sense of gratitude toward this man who had come to make solid his vague wish to become an oceanographer, to give it class and tangibility, like bronzing a baby's shoe. He often felt as though he were the only senior in the world without a college major. And now *he* was going to have one too.

The stranger had on a gray tweed coat and brown pants. He wore a red and gray checked shirt without a tie, and either his socks were flesh-colored or he wore none. His nose and mouth were heavy, his thick-lidded eyes somewhat bulging, as though he spent a lot of time five hundred feet down studying fish, and was unaccustomed to a single atmospheric pressure.

Vaguely disappointed, Eric was startled into attention when the reptilian eyes rose unexpectedly to seize him. There was such keen, focused intelligence in them that he was abashed. He looked down quickly and wrote in his notebook: Dr. Crabtree. Then he underlined it.

Mr. Brown introduced the speaker, who rose. Eric saw clearly, now, that he wore no socks.

"I'm, uh—my specialty . . ." Dr. Crabtree began. He turned and wrote on the board, *Invertebratology*. "I'll more or less have to confine myself to invertebratology," he stated.

Haltingly, he began explaining his business.

So what if he isn't a good speaker? Eric thought.

Dr. Crabtree said that you went to some place like the Indian Ocean or the Aleutians, spent the summer towing a fine-meshed net behind a boat, then spent a couple of years classifying the specimens you caught. While you towed for plankton, other scientists on the ship were taking water samples and ocean-floor corings and labeling them.

Eric smelled a lot of dry detail work. In the lab there was a jar of unclassified plankton that looked like chop suey. He would hate to spend a couple of years unscrambling *that* stuff. But he rallied, thinking of dolphins, and of trapping fish specimens in tropical waters with a slurp-gun.

Finally it was time for questions.

"How does a dolphin stay underwater so long?" Eric asked quickly.

Dr. Crabtree frowned. "Actually, I'm not qualified to hazard a statement about that. It really isn't my field."

"Make a guess," called Henry Nishamura brashly.

"I'd rather not," the invertebratologist said. "If it got back to our dolphin man that I'd told you, I'd be in the soup. This is something delphinologists themselves don't know, you see—"

Eric rallied and asked why it did not crush a dolphin to dive so deep.

Dr. Crabtree patted his pockets as though he had temporarily misplaced a book called *1001 Answers*. He gave a troubled smile. He said the answer was not definitely known, and he was not the one to speculate.

Henry Nishamura then asked why the hammerhead shark had his eyes out on horns that way? Dr. Crabtree said he did not know, and doubted that anyone else did. Species adaptation of some sort. Interesting question, though.

A girl wanted to know why there was no kelp in the Gulf of California. At last Dr. Crabtree came out with a flat answer: The water was too warm.

He fielded other questions as nervously as a center fielder catching fungoed hand grenades. When the bell rang, he seemed to feel a sort of apology was in order.

"I'm sorry I couldn't be more specific," he said. "But the age of the all-around scientist is over. A Renaissance man could grasp in his lifetime all that was known about most of the sciences. Now it's impossible. It's the age of the micro-specialist."

Or the mini-expert, thought Eric, sunk in gloom. All he understood now that he had not when the hour started was that it was major-changing time again.

Eric sat between Henry Nishamura and Flip Stafford in the cafeteria. Henry recognized quickly that Eric was way down emotionally, and moved in quickly. He was a sturdy boy with a second-generation Japanese-American build—strong, fairly tall, sturdy. He wore horn-rimmed glasses and had his hair clipped to the skull. The son of a successful farmer, he liked to needle the Ranch kids.

"How'd you like Crabtree?" he asked Eric. Then he gave his laugh, a burst of merriment from a Gatling gun in his chest.

Eric wagged his head. "He really torpedoed me, man. When do we have to send out our college applications?"

"Pretty soon, man, pretty soon. What's it going to be this time?"

"Spanish studies, maybe. It might be a kick to be an interpreter at the UN."

Flip Stafford, a small, dark, good-looking boy from the Ranch, said, "They'd need another interpreter to put your border Spanish into Castilian."

"You guys've got some points to make up before you go to any college, haven't you?" Henry said. "Say about a year of summer school?"

Flip pulled something from his pocket. "Glad you mentioned that!" On the table he laid a brochure with a cover showing a snowy cruise ship sailing into a blue-green tropical harbor.

"How's *that* for a summer school?" he said to Eric. "That's me standing on the bow of that ship with a Smith College babe beside me!"

"You mean some college babe named Smith," jeered Henry.

As Eric read the brochure, his ears stiffened with pleasure, as though the girl in the picture had run her fingernail down his bare back. S.S. *Summer School of the Seas,* it said. A blur of place-names—Costa Rica, Santiago, Portugal—fogged his brain.

"You hit all these great ports, make up what you need for college entrance, and get full credit!" Flip said. "It's all settled with my folks. I'm going."

"Accredited by all major colleges, such as Iceland School of Mines and Moultrie College of Embalming?" Henry said. He slapped the table and roared out another laugh.

"Can I borrow this brochure?" Eric asked. "I think I'll go too."

"Okay, but you'd better get your application in pretty soon," Flip said. "The director told my mother the roster is nearly full."

"How about you guys coming over tonight?" Eric said hastily, as the bell rang. "I'll do your Spanish, Hank, and you can do my biology. Flip can sell my mother on this summer school deal. Bring your instruments and we'll pick and sing awhile."

"Isn't this Daddy's Train Night at your pad?" Henry asked, with a grin.

Eric suddenly realized it was. Three Mothball Admiral friends of his father's came over one night each week to play with the giant electric train layout in the basement. Visitors were barred. The men took it so seriously that, more often than not, they wound up shouting at each other. It was not the perfect night for a picking and singing session; but it was important to launch the S.S. *Summer School* and see if it floated.

"Be okay," Eric said. "As long as we stay out of the basement. About seven-thirty, huh?"

All at once he felt good again. He was going to spend the

summer on a cruise ship and he was coming back with a commitment to something, and maybe even a college girl committed to him! Hot dog!

At 3:05, he limped into Coach Martin's office. "I think I pulled a ligament last night, Coach," he said. "Had I better run today?"

"Hell, no! Put the heat lamp on it and use some of that salve I gave you."

"All right. We've got a heat lamp at home. About a half-hour?"

"At least. You'd better be in shape by Saturday, Hansen. Frankly, I think that Oceanside kid is going to make you look silly anyway. You're not the man you were last year."

Eric ground a fist into his palm, grinning. "Bet your last buck on this baby, Coach," he said.

He limped around the corner of the gym, then exploded into a sprint that landed him on the bus just before it pulled out.

chapter **3**

The bus dropped six youngsters, including Eric, in the Village, which consisted of a post office, a grocery store, a ranchy-looking gas station and Porsche agency, and a quadrangle of shops scattered around an expanse of brick paving. Enormous eucalyptus trees dropped their leaves, their thin-skinned bark, and their shade everywhere.

There was also the Coffee Shop, where Eric and the others headed as soon as they dropped off the bus. Eric was anxious to talk to Mabel about what had happened at Cresswell's last night. Mabel was a sort of hollow tree where scraps of information were exchanged. He figured she probably knew all about it by now, Sergeant Harris having a mouth big enough for two cops. Maybe she could explain to him what to do about delinquent parents.

From behind the horseshoe counter, Mabel gave him a special look, and a wink. Eric's pulse jumped: she knew something! Taking orders, she moved about with the calm, slow power of a lady shot-putter. She was solidly built but not fat, with reddish hair worn boyishly short, and handsome features. When she brought Eric's root beer float, she murmured,

"Want to see you before you leave, Champ."

Eric swilled the root beer down thirstily, reflecting. The great thing about Mabel was that you could actually *talk* to her about things that mattered to you. Her eyes never glazed over with disinterest the way his parents' did. "My gosh!" she would say, as you told her something, or, "Holy cow, you said *that?*"

With Mabel you could unravel like fifty feet of thread, and she would somehow get you back on your spool again. Just how, Eric wasn't sure. She seldom gave advice, merely listened and made a comment now and then. ("Joanie did that? Well, you know what would kill the little snip? If you didn't even let on. Believe me, Champ, I know women!")

She was good with kids' problems, all right. But he had never tried her out on those of delinquent adults.

Dawdling over his drink, he was the last to finish. The café was empty but for him when Mabel came over.

"How's your father, Rick?" she asked.

"Okay, I guess. Why?"

Mabel began dipping glasses in rinse water. "He came here from the doctor's office this morning. All he wanted was a glass of water to take a pill. It was a little one no larger than a BB, like a heart pill. I just wondered—"

"That's a new one," Eric said. "Did he seem okay?"

"Physically, but he had a lot on his mind. What happened last night?" Mabel asked.

Eric studied her face. "What'd you hear happened?"

Mabel gave a pained smile. "Sergeant Harris should have his mouth taped. He told me he caught your father tearing out bricks and mixing mortar in Cresswell's new house last night! He said Mr. Hansen was very uncooperative. That he even cursed him!"

"Aw, that old flatfoot!" Eric snorted. "I know what Dad was doing, now. He was *redesigning* the fireplace."

And he told her about his father's being bothered by the fireplace design. But it still sounded pretty eccentric.

"It's an interesting hobby," Mabel commented. "Redesigning other people's fireplaces by flashlight . . ."

Gloomily, Eric made a gurgling sound with his straw. In a way it was worse than vandalism, he thought. It was a compulsion.

"He and I'd had a hassle last night," he admitted. "Maybe he was laying bricks to get the feeling off him. You know?"

"Uh-huh. But my gosh, Champ, he can't go around altering houses he doesn't like!"

"Actually, I'm kind of worried about him," Eric confessed. "He's all wound up and getting worse. He used to be a ball. . . ."

He talked about how it was when he was ten or eleven. Mr. Hansen had just acquired a patent on an ingenious pair of pliers he called the HanDeeRench, and he rented an old factory building in San Diego and started manufacturing them. After that the money never quit. Soon they moved to Rancho Sereno and switched to bigger cars.

But as busy as his father was, he found time to be interested in everything. Eric had felt whetted by his enthusiasm. Touch him and you got a tiny jolt of electricity. Then only ten, he knew that if he threw any kind of ball at him he would immediately get a game going.

It was that way until he sold the plant, Eric told Mabel. Then, overnight, things changed.

"It was like trying to gear himself down from being a Grand Prix champion to driving a taxicab," he mused. "He's been bored stiff ever since. Oh, he messes around with things like that tuna boat we owned a share of—the *Santa Ynez:* it sank off Central America—and the quarter horses we raised, and all that junk. And the grove! What a loser! But he's just spinning his wheels. And the electric trains! It used to be *my* train layout. Now I'm not even allowed in the basement. They've got thousands of dollars in equipment down there. And all he and his pals do is bitch at each other when they run the trains."

Mabel dunked another glass. "What about this argument you and he had?"

"He wanted me to run last night, and I was too tired. Plus, he was sore because I took down the motorcycle and haven't put it back together yet."

With a smile, Mabel said, "I think you *do* have a little problem with procrastination, Rick."

Eric rubbed his forehead. "Yeah, I guess." Guess? He knew darned well he had. The fact was, nothing seemed quite important enough to finish, somehow. And with the maid, Cruz, around to pick up after him, and his father to take care of his mechanical problems, well—I don't know, he thought, I guess I'm just lazy. Just the way I am, he decided.

"Retirement was your father's big mistake," Mabel agreed. "He's a big man with a lot of energy. He ought to buy some rundown business and build it up."

"Tell him that!" Eric urged. "I can't. He wouldn't listen to me."

"I'll tell you a secret," said Mabel, smiling wryly. "Your father wouldn't listen to me, either. But he's a guy that needs to be tackling problems other people shy away from. Like last week I told him my car kept stalling, so he borrowed my keys and came back a half-hour later grinning and covered with grease. 'It won't stall now,' he said. 'Some idiot set your carburetor too lean. Your engine mounts were loose, too,' he told me. 'I tightened them up for you.' "

Eric nodded. "He's the Florence Nightingale of broken-down machinery," he agreed. "No offense meant to your car, Mabel. If he'd just get into some business . . ."

Drying her hands on a towel, Mabel said, "I'll give it some thought, Rick. I really feel like he'd better get involved with something pretty soon, or he's going to wind up doing time for tearing down houses."

Eric left. He thought of calling his mother to come after him, but, feeling guilty about breaking training, he decided to jog home. It was a two-and-a-half-mile run. Bridle paths paralleled the road most of the way. Two men in a golf cart were heading for the road crossing at a point where the blacktop cut through the golf course. Swinging a book in each hand, Eric speeded up.

"If I can't beat that cart," he thought suddenly, "that Oceanside High kid will take me Saturday!"

He was already running faster than his normal pace, but now he shook his stride out to the limit. He had recently taken to playing this *If I Can't* game in his head. It worried him slightly. He would tell himself, *If I Can't beat that horse to the intersection, I'll never get into a college!* Or, *I'll lose on Satur-*

day! It bothered him that he should take the contests so seriously, like placing real bets on merry-go-round horses.

In the last fifteen seconds, the cart lost power on the hill and Eric crossed ahead of it. Exhausted, Eric sat down beside the road to rest.

"Your face is so red, Dad," Eric's mother said at dinner. "Did you play golf today?"

"No."

Eric's father kept silently forking in the food. Dinner was late because Mrs. Hansen had come in at six from playing tennis and it was the maid's day off. She was still in shorts and tennis blouse, with a white band around her hair, a small, ash-blonde woman, very tan.

"Gosh, Dad, you look like a lobster!" Debbie exclaimed. She was already taller than her mother, a slender copy of her, very pretty except for the elaborate braces she wore.

"Thanks, Deb," said Mr. Hansen tersely.

Mrs. Hansen touched his forehead. "Why, you're feverish!" she exclaimed.

Slamming his hand down on the table, Mr. Hansen said, "Can we get off my red face for a minute? Is this a clinic or a dinner table?"

Everyone stared at him.

"Well, *excuse* us," Mrs. Hansen said and gave a little laugh. "I just thought if you have a temperature maybe you ought to call Dr. Edwards."

"I'm all right, woman," Mr. Hansen muttered. "How was the tennis?"

Mrs. Hansen clapped her hands. "I won all three sets! Marge was wild! She actually threw her racket into the fence after the third set."

"Mother! Really?" said Debbie. "She's as bad as Tina at the last horse show."

Tina was Marge's daughter. There was some woman talk about the Fleming women as poor losers. Then:

"This is train night, isn't it?" Mrs. Hansen asked.

"Uh-huh."

"Will you put a flea in George Krebs's ear for me? The Trails Committee decided last night to keep after him until we get that bridle path easement. If he should decide to plant trees in the path, there's nothing whatever to stop him."

"What am I supposed to do?" asked Eric's father.

"Talk to him. He'll listen to you if he'll listen to anybody."

Mr. Hansen inspected a forkful of food, appearing sardonically amused by it. "Think of something you've got that George wants, and suggest a trade. How about horse manure? The Riding Club owns tons of it. Great move for his grove."

He grinned. Eric's radar took a sweep and reported enemy activity suddenly diminished: conditions were favorable for mentioning the S.S. *Summer School of the Seas*. He got the brochure from his pocket and laid it on the table. But Debbie's radar was operating too; she was there a split second ahead of him.

"Am I going to have to wear that old green sack to the cotillion next week, Mom?" she asked.

"You've only worn it once, sweetie," said her mother.

"Mom, green isn't my color! We *decided* that. And besides it was too tight over the hips. I was a mess."

"Whadja expect, Fatso?" Eric asked. "You shovel in the food like a longshoreman."

"Yeah, *you're* so handsome!" sneered Debbie. "Front teeth cracked, skinny legs—"

"Anybody want to know what I did today?" Eric's father interrupted. There was an expectant attention.

"Of course," said Eric's mother pleasantly.

"I decided to go back into business."

Eric lowered his fork and waited, startled.

Mrs. Hansen raised her brows. She uttered a nervous little laugh. "Go *back* into business? You've never gotten out."

"I mean full-time, like any other working stiff." Mr. Hansen broke into a grin. Vitality glowed on him like a halo. "The darndest thing!" he said. "I was talking to Pancho Vincent today, and I said I thought I'd get back into something that took up more of my time—"

Eric's mother cut in with a laugh, still smiling but with pained lines about her eyes.

"More of your time!" she crowed. "Like twenty-four hours a day? You're only on the church board, oversee the grove, do our taxes and investments—"

She kept talking, but Eric perceived that his father had tuned her out. He tingled with delight. It was as if his father had picked up his and Mabel's thought waves. Fantastic!

"Shut up, woman," said Mr. Hansen. "I'm just horsing around, and you know it. So Pancho said, 'Why don't you buy my car agency?' and I said, 'Since when is it for sale?' And he said, 'Since next week. I've been thinking of getting out of the auto business.' How about that?" he asked.

Beaming, he gazed around the table.

Eric reached out and offered his hand. They shook. Something happened in that instant: they actually looked at each other. Eric was carried back to the first time they had gone into the ocean together, years ago, and got dumped by a wave and came up gasping and laughing—to look at each other in the same rare, delighted way: making contact.

He said, "Beautiful! You could really straighten out that garage. Pancho's men aren't mechanics, they're just paid vandals."

"Be quiet a minute, Eric," his mother said curtly. "You have to be kidding," she told her husband earnestly. "Where in heaven would you squeeze in another business?"

"Well, I might start by pulling out of some of the Mickey Mouse things I'm doing now. It's a good franchise, even if Pancho runs the agency like a stockyard."

"Oh, fine!" Debbie came in. "So when kids ask me, 'What does your father do?' I can say, 'He's a grease monkey.' "

"I agree that Pancho is a dolt," Mrs. Hansen said. "But that's all the more reason why you shouldn't get involved in an agency with a bad reputation."

Sitting back in his chair, Eric's father shrugged. "I'll live it down. Before I get through, people will be coming to me on purpose—not because it's the only garage within ten miles."

He was still smiling; but, with a throb of anxiety, Eric detected a tiny cloud of doubt forming.

"Darling, I don't mean to knock it," said Eric's mother. "If I thought it were a good idea, I'd be as keen on it as you. But —well—just for instance. Suppose you worked on George Krebs's car, and he wasn't satisfied? It would drive a little wedge between you and him. And after all, most of your business would be with people you know."

Mr. Hansen gave an impatient hand-wave, as though trying to dissipate an annoying cloud of cigar smoke. "That's what I'm trying to tell you, woman. When I work on a car, people are going to drive out with a smile on their faces."

"Oh, I see. You're going to be the mechanic? So who's going to be running the business end of the operation?"

Eric saw a wrinkle of confusion come between his father's eyes. Mr. Hansen said, "I am. Naturally, I won't be in the pits myself. I'll act as service manager until I can find and train a good man. After that—"

"After that," his wife said, "the show will be over. Why did you sell the HanDeeRench plant? Because you had it running so well there was nothing to do but sign papers. You liked it while it was small and you could be into everything. But when it got big, and you had no excuse for fiddling around in the shop, you were bored with it. Isn't that true?"

Mr. Hansen rubbed his forehead hard with two fingers, as though he could erase the idea she had written on his brain. Eric felt dull and dispirited. It was over. What made him so discouraged was that she was probably right.

"Well, yes," his father grumbled, "but—"

"You can get all the mechanical kicks you want out of your hobbies."

"Sure, Dad," Debbie said, looking pleased. "Your trains, and your sports car—"

"What time are the men coming, by the way?" asked Mrs. Hansen.

"Eight."

"Don't forget about George—the easement. All right?"

Mr. Hansen growled agreement.

Mrs. Hansen brought dessert. The coconut cake seemed to sweeten Eric's father's spirits a bit, but feeling that torpedo danger to the S.S. *Summer School* remained great, Eric started to slide the brochure from the table.

"What's that?" his father asked, rousing from his torpor.

"Ummm—travel brochure. Flip—"

"Let's see it." Mr. Hansen liked Flip. But after glancing over the folder, he snorted. "Ridiculous," he said.

Nettled, Eric retorted, "Flip's going. His folks thought it was a great idea."

"Is that a fact?" said Mr. Hansen. He tossed the folder on the table. "Well, you're not going."

chapter **4**

"Level with us, Eric," Henry Nishamura said. "Do they really wear train hats?"

The boys, finished with their homework, had sat for a half-hour on the floor eating corn chips and picking and singing bluegrass songs. Two stories below, in the locked basement of the house, Mr. Hansen and his friends were playing with their trains.

"Who said they wear train hats?" Eric said.

"Everybody. Mabel told me once that George Krebs even wears engineer's overalls."

"Maybe he does. I've never been down there when they were working. No visitors allowed."

"What do they do?" asked Flip. "Just run the trains around the floor?"

"Are you kidding? They make up work orders during the week. Each man has a lot of stuff to move. They have to observe regulation train rules, and the one that gets back to his station first gets points—or something."

The other boys grinned. Eric, feeling that he had to defend his father's honor, added,

"They do it so realistically that a big toy company gives them miniaturized equipment to test."

"How many cars do they have?" asked Henry.

"Dad's got six locomotives and I guess about thirty cars."

"Wow! Do you ever get to play with them?"

"Oh, sure. And my mother lets me write on windows with her diamonds. One of those locos is worth a couple of hundred bucks, man. Dad let me run a passenger train for a few minutes about a year ago, but I ran into a closed switch and he threw me out."

. . . He remembered the layout, like a child's vision of flying, a dreamlike world of miniature hills, valleys, a lake, even a small city. The men took their play so seriously that, more often than not, an argument was going on when they left.

"Why don't we kind of ease down the stairs and watch for a while?" Henry asked.

"If they see us," said Flip, quickly, "you can fake it—tell your dad you wanted to ask whether he'd give a Careers talk or something."

Eric pushed a handful of corn chips in his mouth. "In the first place," he mumbled, "the basement's probably locked."

"Probably?" Henry said.

"They always used to keep it locked, but I don't know if they still do."

"Let's find out, huh?"

"No, man. Believe me, it would be a bad idea. By now, everybody's probably sore at Krebs. I heard Wendell Drake yell at him one night, 'You act like a damned pirate, George, just like you did in the construction business!'"

"Crazy!" Henry said. "Come on, Rick-baby—they won't see us."

"Well, I don't know . . ." Eric said; but as he hesitated he thought of the blunt turndown on the S.S. *Summer School*. He grinned and laid his guitar aside. It was a small matter, after all. "Okay, men. But lemme tell you—the biggest favor we can do ourselves is not to get caught."

They stole like thieves down the stairs to the living room. The basement door was at the far end of the room. Reaching the bottom of the stairs, Eric headed for a heat register in the corner to check sounds rising from the basement. Abruptly, seeing a man standing behind the bar near the register, he froze.

"Ah, ha!" said the man. "The famous singing liquor thieves strike again!"

Flip recovered first and said, "It's just a soft-drink heist tonight, Mr. Hansen."

Liquor or trains had infused Mr. Hansen with good humor. "Help yourselves," he said heartily. He finished mixing drinks and placed them on a tray.

"You've lost some weight," Flip said, with his Parents Smile. "You're looking good."

Mr. Hansen patted his stomach. "Maybe a pound—but thanks. Say, Rick, I think a cat's stuck in the heat system. We've been hearing the darndest caterwauling."

The boys laughed. Eric's father drove a cork in a bottle

with his fist and crossed the room to the basement door, carrying the tray of drinks. He went through, closing it behind himself.

"Close!" Henry said.

"How long do we have to wait?" Flip asked.

"Few minutes. We'll hear the trains again."

They drank Cokes and waited. Eric lay on the floor beside the heat register. He could hear a mumble of voices, a tinkle of ice. Suddenly a bell rang. An instant later a man's voice said:

"Dammit, George, you jumped the gun again!"

"Anybody can be slow," came the truculent bass voice of George Krebs.

Eric scrambled up and tiptoed across the floor. Painstakingly he opened the basement door. The stairs were anchored to a concrete wall on the right. On the left was a plaster partition; where it ended, the squarish bulk of the furnace made a screen. With a gesture commanding silence, he started down.

At the foot of the stairs hung a veil of typical cellar-shadows. Old Hallowe'en costumes drooped from hooks along the wall, among trunks, travel posters, and demolished couches. He hesitated at the bottom, then moved out along the wall, stopping with the big room at his left. The other boys moved up beside him. The train layout was now in clear view, looking like a giant relief map on trestles.

Starting about fifteen feet from where they stood, the world of the little trains ran from side wall to side wall, with a U cut into the huge table to allow the trainmen to be more or less in the heart of the diorama. Seated on high stools within this section, the four trainmen were hunched over individual consoles of buttons and lights. All wore tall trainmen's caps of blue and white ticking. In addition, George Krebs, a very tall cranelike man with sour coppery features, was dressed in trainmen's overalls.

"Holy tomato!" Henry whispered.

Eric saw his father's blue-and-yellow Santa Fe cars plunge out of sight into a tunnel. Somewhere there was a feisty blaring of a tiny diesel horn. Who had blown it? he wondered.

Two other strings of cars were gliding snakelike through groves, one wearing the colors of the old New York Central line, another those of the Pennsylvania Railroad. On converging tracks, these trains seemed to be hurrying toward a collision at a complex of packing houses. On the roof of one building were the words, SunGold Citrus.

Again Eric heard the horn. This time he saw Wendell Drake, a gaunt gray-haired man, stabbing at a button on his control panel; it was his New York Central locomotive that was blaring in mouselike fury.

"Dammit, George," Wendell cried, "I've got right-of-way at the packing house!"

"You have if you get there first, buddy," said Krebs.

"Read your work orders, George! You were supposed to drop that Nickel Plate gondola at Peachtree siding."

"Rick was still on the siding. I'll drop it at SunGold and take it back with a yard goat after I finish my run."

"You can't do that!" Wendell cried. "What the hell good are rules if you're going to break them whenever you're behind?"

Eric's father laughed. His locomotive, emerging from the tunnel, was now running alongside a lake in a far corner of the layout. "Come on, guys. Fletch, you're the lawyer, what do you say?"

Young Fletcher Hamilton smiled as he maneuvered his own cars up to a raised drawbridge. A retired lawyer of thirty-two, his main contribution, Mr. Hansen had once told Eric, was to keep the other men from clawing each other's guts out.

"In my opinion," said Fletch, "an appraisal of the situation is definitely in order. Shall we call a recess?"

Wendell said grumpily, "I'll stop if he will."

But Krebs fed his locomotive even more juice, immediately seizing the lead in the race. Wendell Drake responded by jerkily twisting a rheostat.

"Cut it out!" he shouted. "You're going at least a hundred and ten!"

Krebs's face toughened. "So what? I'm running light."

"Not that light! Give way!"

The boys shivered with excitement. Flip whispered anxiously, "Jeez, they're really going to cream each other!"

"Nah," Eric whispered. "They always fight like this. But Wendell always gives way."

The cars were racing through the groves on a certain collision course. Lights began to blink along the right-of-way. Semaphores snapped up near the SunGold packing house. A warning bell jangled. Fletch Hamilton, with a nervous gesture, called out,

"Gentlemen, if I may venture an opinion . . . !"

"Come on, George," said Eric's father. "Be nice. After all, you *didn't* make that stop—"

"Stay out of this," snarled Krebs. "You're the one who blocked me at the siding, so who the hell are you lecturing?"

Flip gripped Eric's arm. "They're going to crash, Rick! Why doesn't somebody turn off the juice?"

Eric made a thumb gesture at the wall. "There's the fuse box, if you can't stand the suspense."

Not really disturbed, he watched with the pleasant anguish of one observing a savage fight on television, knowing that the bottles being broken over bare heads were of spun sugar, that the blood flowing so freely was paint.

Then, true to form, he saw Wendell flinch and begin to turn a knob. Krebs's string was slightly ahead, and if there were to be a collision it would consist in Wendell's locomotive crashing into Krebs's car. Wendell was cutting it close, making Krebs sweat and bringing a curse from his lips.

"So help me," Krebs cried. "If you . . . !"

"I'm coming through!" Wendell retorted.

"Look out!" Flip yelled.

Eric stiffened in horror. Flip darted to the fuse box a few feet away, as the men turned in astonishment. Krebs raised his hands above his head, as though prepared to surrender his wallet. Wendell made an involuntary motion on the control panel and his locomotive leaped ahead at full power. Horrified, Eric saw sparks—a flash—cars and pieces of cars in the air. Gondola after gondola heaped with tiny oranges flipped over. Bluish smoke rose.

The lights went out.

Something was rolling around on the floor like a piepan. Men were shouting. *"What the hell . . . !"* There was a splintering crash; Eric guessed that one of the control panels had toppled to the floor. He turned and bolted up the stairs.

chapter **5**

In the living room, Eric stood shaking like a malaria victim. Flip and Henry had gasped out promises to call later and gone rushing away into the night. He heard Flip's car departing. In a moment, four demented trainmen would charge from the basement like lions looking for a Christian to devour.

"Eric?" His mother had materialized at the head of the stairs. "What happened? I thought I heard you boys really whooping it up."

It was on his lips to blurt it all out and run upstairs to his room. A great tactician, his mother could handle the men better than he could. But he was ashamed to let her field their line drives for him.

He could hear shouts in the basement, then someone on the stairs. The sounds freed him.

"Something happened—a short!" he said. "I'll turn off the power . . ." He hurried to the door of the game room, then sprinted through to the back door. He heard her call, but was out the door quickly and running down the walk.

He was bursting with reactions but empty of plans. Glancing down the hill toward the county road, he saw the boys' taillights vanishing. In panic, he gazed up a work road winding through the lemon grove to a ridge. He broke into a run. Arms pumping, he charged past the garage and headed up the rutted dirt road. In a couple of minutes, winded, he reached a brushy ridge above the house and sat down to rest. Lights burned throughout the house. Men bayed in the yard like bloodhounds. He pictured them running around in their train hats beating the shrubbery for him.

His body raced with excitement and an itchy feeling of triumph. Yet he knew he had taken a long leap, a dive into an empty pool, and when he hit bottom he was going to feel some shock waves. There would have been a wreck anyway, but now, thanks to Flip, the trainmen had a scapegoat. He had broken a law in a world run by idiots, and would have to take his punishment. The gas chamber for overparking.

The night was moonless, but reflected light made the stones appear luminously white. He heard crickets, randomly tuned and sounding like an army of tiny bell ringers in the brush. A shooting star blazed out of the Milky Way, holding out a mystical promise.

If that star makes it to the horizon, everything will be okay, he thought, prayerfully. But the star burned to a clinker before his eyes.

After some time he heard a car start and saw ruby taillights twisting down the drive. Now his father would sit down to wait, like a manhunter who knew his prey would have to come to him. The sense of injustice trickled through Eric like acid. On impulse, he got up and started jogging along the ridge. He would go to the Village and call Joanie Carlson. Joanie had her own telephone, so her mother wouldn't get in on the conversation. He hungered to talk to someone on his wavelength.

Sweating lightly in the cool night, he reached the darkened Village. Everything was buttoned up, the neon signs cold, night lights burning lonesomely in the shops. The Coffee Shop was closed. He crossed the slick cement forecourt of Pancho Vincent's auto agency to the telephone booth near the gas pumps. As his dime dropped and the little bell rang, his spirits lifted.

Joanie answered with a puzzled "Hello?", as though she had been saying it and no one had answered.

"Hi. Were you asleep?"

"Oh, hi. No. Gee, I'm glad you called! Did Flip tell you about that summer school cruise?"

"Yes, but—"

"Isn't it groovy? Are you going?"

"I was thinking of going, but now it's out. I've got a little problem. Old Flipper really messed me up—"

And in a long, backtracking manner, he told her about the Great Train Wreck. Every now and then she would say, "Oh, no!" or "My stars!" or one of the expressions he had heard her mother use.

". . . I could cut Flip's throat!" he said, winding it up. "But what really fries me is that *they've* got the train compulsion, but *I* get the shaft when one of them snaps his cap! They play together like a bunch of spoiled kids."

"But it *is* their hobby, Eric," said Joanie.

"You know it is! And they lock people up for having hobbies like that. They're a bunch of psychos."

"But just because *you* don't like their hobby—I mean, I know how you feel, but . . ."

He listened to her explaining it, his steam rising again. She did not seem to get the idea at all; he was asking for a fire extinguisher, not a lecture on dousing your campfire.

"And besides, look who they are," she finished. "Mr. Krebs was a *very* successful construction man, and Fletch Hamilton was a *great* lawyer—"

"He was a great phony, like all the rest of them. They're all phonies!"

"I don't think you have any right saying that. Maybe you—"

"Shut up for a minute, will you?" Eric was so angry that he could not speak without gasping. What she failed to realize was that sometimes a girl was supposed to just shut up and listen.

"I mean—well, it's like some backwoods town made it a capital offense to run a stoplight," he said. "It's not that big a deal!"

"Apparently it is to them," said Joanie primly.

"It isn't to me."

"Why don't you just tell your father that, then? Maybe he'll take up some other hobby."

"Very funny. You Pridmore girls are a panic. And another thing—he may sell my motorcycle." Outraged, he told her about it. But Joanie said nothing. "How do you like that?" he said, inviting support.

"I don't know enough about it to say. All I know is that you can't fight the Establishment. Do you want to know what I'd do?"

"What would you do?"

"I'd call them all right now and apologize. Then when you get home your father will at least know you're sorry."

"Thanks a heap," Eric said bitterly. "I could get that kind of advice from George Krebs."

Snarling, he hung up. He kicked the door open. There was no big love thing between him and Joanie, but she could at least have acted as if she were on his team. Hands shoved in his pockets, he plodded from the Village toward home, and his fate.

His father was shooting pool in the game room, a drink resting on the table's edge. Eric slumped onto the couch. Mr. Hansen made a couple of shots without saying anything. At last he sat down with the drink.

"Great play, Rick," he said. "Perfectly amazing."

"I'm sorry. Didn't you ever make a mistake?"

"Undoubtedly. Maybe not quite as big as this. This was a classic."

Eric blinked at his feet, frowning.

"Flip called and took the blame for the wreck," his father said. "Kid's got class. But who took him down there?"

Eric kept blinking and frowning.

"Well, say something! Defend yourself."

Eric looked up sullenly. "I think the whole train bit is pretty stupid. And if you didn't think so too, you wouldn't have such a big security thing about no visitors."

He sensed a hesitation before his father said, "We've got thousands of dollars invested down there, and visitors can't keep their hands off things—as you see. The work takes concentration, too."

"They're still toys, aren't they?"

"In the strictest sense. But—"

"It was just my lousy luck that we sneaked in tonight, because there was going to be a wreck regardless. It's been coming for months. Mabel says—"

He closed his mouth. His father stared at him. "Yeah, what's Mabel say?"

"She's always said that Krebs was going to flip his wig sooner or later."

"Maybe you'd better hire Mabel as your lawyer."

"She's got Krebs psyched out, at least. And all the other Mothball Admirals around here—that's what she calls them."

With his glass at his lips, Mr. Hansen lowered it. "The what?"

Eric slumped deeper, his hands working in his pockets. "The retired guys. She calls them Admirals of the Mothball Fleet."

"Very clever. Has she explained to you how they were *able* to retire here and enjoy life?"

Knowing better, since it was unbecoming for those copping a guilty plea to try to score points, Eric said,

"How about Fletch Hamilton?"

His slightly drunken eyes cold, his father said, "Fletcher Hamilton was a junior partner with Hayes, Thomas, and Reed before he retired."

"But he didn't retire until his wife's rich aunt died. Flip's mother says they were practically in hock till then, waiting for the old lady to hang up her spikes."

"I think that may be true. I also think it's their business."

Eric got up and chalked the pool cue.

"I'm talking to you!" his father said.

"I'm listening!" Eric laid the cue down.

"What does the sage of Rancho Sereno have to say about Hansen, of HanDeeRench Pliers fame?"

Eric sulked a moment, then shrugged. "She thinks you should have kept the plant. She says you're the kind that needs to stay busy."

"Busy! Does May-Belle think the grove runs itself? Our stocks, investments—they buy and sell themselves?"

Eric rolled a ball across the table. "You were saying tonight," he reminded his father, "that you wanted to buy out Pancho to have *more* to do . . ."

Mr. Hansen's eyes faltered as though he had taken a solid one in the stomach. He had forgotten that a few hours ago he had been orating on the other school's debating team.

"Your mother was quite right," he said. "I'm into too many things already. And I don't want an eighteen-hour-a-day setup again. I'm too busy as it is."

Quietly Eric rolled another ball, feeling his father's stare on him.

"Well, what?" his father challenged.

"Nothing," said Eric.

"Come on, spit it out! You were grinning about something."

"I was thinking about last night."

"*What* about last night, dammit?"

"About Cresswell's fireplace."

He glanced up and saw his father miss a beat. He was sorry he had said it, though it was the clincher. What he feared suddenly was that his father might burst into tears, or kill him, or something. It was too neat a stroke; a humiliating no-hitter.

Mr. Hansen's ice tinkled. Staring into the glass, he shook it vigorously as though he might jar a little more Scotch out of the cubes.

"Where'd you hear about that? Has Sergeant Bigmouth put it on the wire already?"

"I heard you come home. And Mabel said Sergeant Harris mentioned it today. So it seemed to me that you probably don't have enough to do. Otherwise I shouldn't think you'd be worrying about other people's fireplaces."

He looked at his father with a shy appeal to him to be honest with himself. In Mr. Hansen's ruddy face there was a cement-colored undertone. He looked actually ill. But, seeming to hold himself in carefully, he said,

"Am I wrong, or were we talking about *your* failings? How did we get on the subject of mine? Though perhaps," he added, "I do need some occupational therapy. So I'll start by rebuilding the motorcycle and putting it on the market. The money it brings in will go toward repairing the damage you caused tonight."

Eric mumbled, "Okay."

"Starting tomorrow you'll knock off the hill-billy music, and surfing, and squirreling around with your buddies, until school is out. While we're talking about the failings of the father, we are faced with the fact that the son will have to go to City College for at least a year before he can get into a university. Maybe that isn't important—you might be able to marry a rich woman, like Fletch. I think you'd find it easier to bag one, though, if you've got a college degree and a job."

He got up, clutched the glass an instant, then without warning hurled it into the fireplace. Both of them stared numbly at the fragments of glass in the ashes. An ice cube spun across the floor. Mr. Hansen then started out, bumping a table as he passed and swearing at it under his breath. *Bombed!* Eric thought. After a safe interval, he turned off the lights and went upstairs to bed.

chapter **6**

Through the next day's classes, Eric was distracted by the
thought that the Hansen household had become a sort of glass
pyramid standing on its apex. At any moment it might topple,
and shatter. Flip and Henry tried to make up for last night's
disaster by buying his lunch—a water pistol to extinguish a
holocaust. They apologized, but it was plain that they thought
the humorous aspects of the incident far outweighed the serious ones.

Eric rode the bus home. Trotting up the drive, he heard the
smooth, snoring song of his motorcycle, a Spanish Ossa. He
discovered the Ossa standing under the jacaranda tree near
the pool, his father in white coveralls straddling it. Mr. Han-

sen listened with an ear cocked as he ran the engine up and down. He saw Eric, and, to Eric's surprise, grinned, although he did not interrupt his work.

Man! Eric thought. He's hard to figure. How come so happy?

Eric had a snack, afterward studied for two hours. He smelled meat frying. Cruz, the Mexican girl, came to his door.

"Está lista la cena," she said.

"Loco," Eric said. Crazy. Cruz giggled and went away. They had some good talks in border Spanish. It pleased him that, after having Mexican help for years, his parents still had to get him to translate sometimes. He had learned Spanish as a child, from a succession of women named María—María Guadalupe, María Estela, María Cruz.

For some time it had been quiet below his window. After reassembling the motorcycle, Mr. Hansen tuned up his sports car, a little green Riley. In the anxiety of more urgent matters, the tragedy of losing the motorcycle now seemed minor to Eric.

His father entered the room in his coveralls. "The hot water line's out to my bath," he told Eric. "I'll wash up in yours."

When he emerged from the bathroom, he said, "You're right about Krebs. He's as psycho as they come. Mabel told me he was talking about suing me!"

"What for?"

"Poor slob had to call the doctor when his blood pressure went to over two hundred last night. He claims it may have ruptured a blood vessel in one eye. Poppycock! He was blaming that eye on a war injury last month. I think somebody he swindled probably stuck a thumb in it years ago."

Eric grinned. He lifted his hand over his head and rubbed the back of his neck. "Dad, I'm sorry about—"

"Forget it. I'll probably get out of the choo-choo club anyway."

"I hope I didn't . . ."

Arms crossed, Mr. Hansen stood at the window. "The Age of the Button. Push-pull, click, click. Another breakthrough. But we've got the same old problem we always had."

Eric was not sure he followed his line of thought. "What's that?"

"The problem," said his father, "of what it's all about." He stood silent a moment. Then he said, "Listen, Tiger, I've got a yen for seafood. I'm going over to Sorrento Beach and have some abalone at Charlie's. Tell the womenfolk, will you? Turn down an empty mind for me."

Eric blinked. "Okay. But Cruz said dinner's all ready."

Mr. Hansen came to him and solemnly laid both hands on his shoulders. "My boy, when a Scandinavian gets a craving for fish, it's like an Irishman with an urge for whiskey. Did you know, by the way, that man's blood has exactly the same chemical composition as seawater?"

Eric swallowed and said he hadn't known it.

"So this yen may be in part a desire to return to the sea. Might that not be true?"

"Uh-huh," Eric said, bewildered by the zigzagging conversation.

"By the way—I'm not going to sell the Ossa after all," said his father. "I think the changes I make around here—and there'll be some—should start with me."

Eric shook his head. "No, I think you should sell it. I asked for it."

"Nevertheless I owe you something for jarring me out of my long winter's nap. That deal at Cresswell's—that was definitely on the buggy side. Definitely. I knew I was being a fool, but I couldn't stop. It was like standing aside watching myself tear out bricks; but I couldn't quit."

Eric's gaze fell. "I guess everybody gets carried away sometimes. And it *is* a pretty stupid fireplace."

"If it suits Cresswell, though, that's all it has to do. As for me, I'm going to give a lot of thought to the question of why my own fireplace has been giving out so much smoke and so little heat. . . ."

Suddenly he smiled crookedly and put out his hand. Embarrassed, Eric took it.

"I just want to say one thing," said his father. "I'm sorry if this embarrasses you, but I want to get it in the record. I'm quite proud of you, Rick. In all the important things you've got the right instincts. In a way, a son is something a man says about himself, you might say, and I figure you do me credit."

He released Eric's hand. "That's all. School's out." He punched Eric lightly on the jaw and left the room.

Half an hour later, as they were dining, Eric heard the Riley's hot snarl and saw it flash past the dining room windows. It occurred to him that it had taken his father a long time to get going. Also, he had the impression that the little car was crammed full of equipment of some kind.

chapter **7**

Eric woke late and smelled bacon frying. He dressed hurriedly, and, stuffing in his shirttail, loped downstairs. Debbie and his mother were already eating. His sister looked pretty and sulky.

"You're going to miss the bus," she told Eric, "and Mom will have to haul you to school."

"Can I ride my motor today?" Eric asked his mother.

"No. Deb, hurry up; your ride's due. Is Dad getting up?" Mrs. Hansen asked Eric. She was dressed for tennis. "He has a date at ten with his lawyer."

"I didn't hear him."

"Speaking of dates," said Eric's mother, "you have one with Mr. Krebs for lunch tomorrow."

Eric dropped his grapefruit spoon. *"What?"*

Tilting her chin, his mother said, "I called George and told him you'd like to express your regrets personally, and would he have lunch with you at the golf course Saturday?"

Eric smashed his fist down on the table. Silverware and crockery gave a chiming leap. "Why didn't you ask me?" he yelled. "If you think I'm going to have lunch with that old lush just so you can get a bridle path easement out of him—Besides, I'm running in the track meet."

"Now, stop this! You have a date whether you like it or not. I made it for eleven, so you'll still have time to make the track meet." She rose. "I'd better wake up Dad."

Steaming, Eric sat staring at his plate. Tires ground up the drive through the gravel. Debbie tweaked his ear as she ran out. *Krebs! Brother!* he thought. *Over my dead body.*

A minute or two after Debbie left, Mrs. Hansen returned from upstairs and sat down. She picked up her coffee cup, then lowered it again, looking distressed.

"What's the matter?" Eric asked, still sullen.

"Dad didn't come home last night!"

"He didn't?" Eric said blankly.

"His bed is still made and the Riley's gone."

Eric shivered with the touch of a killing draft that blew only in other people's houses; a whisper of mystery and death. He tried to rally, but could not even speak. "Well, come on! What kind of worm are you?" he asked himself.

"Did he say anything to you last night?" Mrs. Hansen asked.

"Only that he was going to eat in Sorrento Beach."

Mrs. Hansen drew a shaky breath. "I—I suppose I'd better call Sergeant Harris—"

Eric's brain began to thaw. "No! He spills everything. . . . Cruz!" he called. The Mexican girl came from the kitchen. "Did the señor say anything to you when he left?" he asked, in Spanish.

"I didn't know he'd come downstairs."

"No, I mean last night. We don't think he came home!"

Cruz put her hands to her cheeks. *"Dulces caramelos!"* she exclaimed.

"Did he say anything to you before he left?" Eric asked.

"No. I saw a lot of things in his car when he drove out, though," Cruz recalled. "There was a fishing pole tied to the side of the car, and heaps of other things."

"Grunion!" Mrs. Hansen exclaimed. "Don't they run on winter nights?"

"You scoop them up by hand, Mom—you don't use tackle. But he might have done some surf casting. And maybe he slept in his car afterward, and hasn't got in gear yet. . . ."

Treasuring the small clue of the fishing pole, his mother had begun to think. "He was in a pretty foul mood after the Great Train Wreck. He might have decided to go fishing for a few days. But he wouldn't have gone without leaving a note."

"Did you look on his desk?"

Mrs. Hansen got up and headed for her husband's office, off the garage. Eric followed. Lined with shelves of technical books and volumes on navigation, horses, fisheries, golf, Baja California, and a dozen other interests, the office was bare of clues.

Like a lump of cold oatmeal in Eric's throat was the possibility that his father might have spun out on one of the many horseshoe turns of the Ranch roads. About every six months some car went out of control and landed in a gully. It was often hours before anyone saw the wreck under the gray-green tangles of brush.

"I'd better take my bike," he said, "and check around. I'll go over to the beaches and see if he's camping out. I'll check with Charlie, too. Dad'll probably call before I get back."

"All right, dear. Be careful!"

Eric rode to Encino, the northernmost of the small beach towns strung like beads on the old Pacific highway, ten miles from the Ranch. The proprietor of the bait and tackle shop said he had closed at five the previous evening, long before Mr. Hansen had left the house. Eric then swung down to the beach. High tide had wiped the driftwood-colored sand as clean as a slate, leaving it unblemished and silky.

Heading south, he swerved through the various camping areas perched on the reddish cliffs above the sea. The season was still early for campers, and no one seemed to be fishing. At last he came to the stretch of low ground where Sorrento Beach lay. Charlie, the fat, depraved-looking proprietor of Charlie's Fireside Tavern, told Eric he had not seen his father the night before.

"You didn't?" Eric said.

"Not for two weeks. What's the rumble?" Charlie was a jolly man with a whiskey-mottled face. "Has he split?"

"Well, uh—we . . ."

Charlie gave him a thumb in the gut. "Think nothing of it, kid. He's a stud, ain't he? It's some broad, probably. He'll be back in a couple of days with a story who'd believe!"

With Charlie's degenerate laughter in his ears, Eric rode off.

One stop remained. Probably, he realized, it should have been the first: the Village Coffee Shop. It was eleven o'clock when he rode in; hardly a pedestrian stirred in the Village. Eric parked before the restaurant and went in, carrying his helmet. Except for Mabel, the place was empty. She looked surprised at seeing him.

"No school today?"

"Not for me," Eric said cryptically, setting his helmet on the counter.

"What's happening?" Mabel asked.

"You haven't seen my father, have you?"

"No. What's up?"

"He's split," Eric said. He took a stool and looked at her. "He went out for dinner last night and never came back. He told me he was going over to Charlie's Fireside Tavern for seafood. But I was just there, and Charlie said he didn't see him."

Mabel gazed thoughtfully at him, then drew a cup of coffee and carried it around to the customers' side of the counter. Taking a stool beside Eric, she said calmly,

"He ate right here, Rick."

"I figured. Did he tell you anything?"

"Just small talk, and not much of that. How do you know he's split? Did he leave a note? Maybe he just got up early and went out somewhere."

"He didn't sleep in his bed. And the Riley's gone. Cruz said she saw a fishing pole tied to the side of the car when he left."

"It sounds to me," Mabel said, "like the man's gone fishing. Any law against that?"

Eric rested his chin on both fists. "I feel pretty rotten about the whole deal, Mabel. Like I'd pushed him into—whatever he's done." He told her about the Great Train Wreck, and needling his father about the fireplace.

"What I keep thinking," he said, "is that he may have been afraid he was losing his mind. He told me last night he realized it was pretty buggy to redesign somebody else's fireplace in the

middle of the night. I've heard of people killing themselves because they thought their minds were going. Haven't you?"

Mabel warily sipped the steaming coffee. "I never heard of
anybody taking a fishing pole along when he went off to do it.
Think he planned to beat himself to death with it?"

"He's had a bad week, and most of it was my fault. *I* took
the guys down to the basement. *I* wouldn't go running with
him. And *I* threw it up to him about the fireplace."

Mabel laughed and laid her arm across his shoulders.
"Don't be ridiculous! The train thing was a mistake, but they
blew it up all out of proportion. And why *should* you run at
midnight if you've got school the next day?"

It was true. Unfortunately, however, it failed to raise the
feeling of guilt from his conscience.

Mabel said, "Let's use our heads. He had a fishing pole and
a lot of camping gear, right?"

Eric turned his head. "How do you know he had camping
gear?"

"I saw it in the car when he parked in front. So we can
assume he wasn't driving up to Los Angeles to visit friends.
Now, where can you go fishing this time of the year?"

"The ocean."

"But he wouldn't have to camp to go ocean fishing—he
could be there in ten minutes. The mountains?"

"Too cold."

"The desert?"

Eric's grin showed large white teeth with a chipped front
tooth. "And catch a mess of desert trout? For fishing you need
water, Mabel." Then an idea blazed inside his head. "Baja!"
he said.

Mabel squinted. "Maybe. But remember, Baja California is
a thousand miles long and has two coastlines."

"But the Pacific side is still pretty wet and windy," Eric

pointed out, "so it would have to be the Gulf side . . ."

Mentally, he flipped through the possibilities. The Lower California peninsula, hanging down from California like a leg, was scarcely a hundred miles wide at its point of greatest width. But, though winter still blew damply on the Pacific side, along the Gulf of California, to the east, it was spring. Every weekend, hordes of Americans drove down to San Felipe, where the water was warm, the air balmy.

He felt positive now that his father had driven down to San Felipe. But why? In doubt, he chewed a knuckle. Despite Mabel's reassurance, he thought it perfectly plausible that a man bent on suicide might decide to go out doing something he took pleasure in, such as fishing. . . .

"I've got a feeling," Mabel said, "that you're right. I don't know how many times your dad's told me about the year he and some other men rented a boat and went pearl diving in the Gulf. Could be he decided to go down there and think some things out."

"All I know," said Eric, sliding off the stool, "is that Mom and I had better get down there and find out—"

"Why don't you leave the poor guy alone?" Mabel protested. "Those airline ads showing the wife whining, 'Take me along to the convention'—they turn my stomach. Hasn't everybody got a right to be alone once in a while? Would you want your parents bird-dogging you every time you left the city limits?"

Eric held his helmet between his palms, gazing at it as though it were a crystal ball. "It's different," he said slowly, "when a person's been doing peculiar things. That fireplace caper—it's just one step from that to wearing sandals and painting 'Jesus Saves' on rocks. I don't think he should be alone."

Mabel laughed and patted him on the back. "Well, maybe

you're right. Let me give you some advice, though—don't take your mother, if you can talk her out of going. He's a grown man, and I don't think he'd let himself be dragged home by his wife, like he'd been a naughty boy."

Riding home, Eric thought of what Mabel had said. In a flash of insight he suddenly perceived that the whole Ranch Sereno game—parties, clubs, feuds, hobbies—was a sort of complex machine designed and manufactured by women—but very inexpertly—so that it took all the time of every man on the Ranch to keep it from flying apart. Soon a pleasurable excitement began to take over. He fantasied the reunion with his father on the beach at San Felipe. No drying stockings, hair curlers, and other woman-stuff for a while. Just camping, skin-diving, living in the sun. He gave a shiver of pure delight.

As he parked the Ossa, his mother came hurrying from the house. Grinning, he waved one hand in salute. "We're in!" he called.

"Did you find him?"

"No, but we think he's at San Felipe."

"We?" His mother frowned.

"I was talking to Mabel. He had dinner at the Coffee Shop last night. She says his car was full of camping gear. Where else can you camp this time of year that you could use a fishing pole?"

His mother nibbled a thumbnail. "It does make sense, doesn't it? Yes, of course. . . . The only thing that worries me—I found a little bottle of pills in the medicine chest after you left. The date on the label was yesterday, so I knew he'd been to the doctor. I called Dr. Edwards, and he said he'd detected a little heart irregularity."

Eric groaned.

"He said he didn't think it was serious, but he'd sent him to a lab for some tests and he's waiting for the report."

"Jeez, we'd better get going!" Eric gulped. Things were rapidly getting worse. If his father didn't kill himself, it began to look as though he'd die a natural death through overexertion.

His mother, making a U-turn in the conversation, asked, "Did you think I was abrupt when I argued against his buying the auto agency?"

"You kind of shot him down," Eric replied.

"I didn't mean to. All I wanted was what was best for him. And I knew exactly how it would go if he bought it."

"Uh-huh," Eric said, himself confused about who was right and who was wrong in that scene. Probably it would have been better, he thought, to have let his father make the mistake, rather than to leave him feeling like a corrected child.

"Lunch is ready," Mrs. Hansen said. As they walked toward the house, she said unexpectedly, "You know, I think it might be better if you went alone. Would you be afraid to?"

"Of what?"

"It *is* a foreign country, and you have to be careful. I have a feeling that he's probably mad at me because I shot him down, as you say. He may be mad at you, too, but you're his son and he'll listen to you, where I'm only his wife."

Eric held back a grin. Strange, he thought, how both Mabel and his mother had sensed what the effect might be on his father if Mrs. Hansen showed up at San Felipe! Women had a kind of radar for such things.

"I think that's a good idea," he said soberly. "I'd better chow down and hit the road. If I'm lucky, I can still be in San Felipe before dark."

"I'll help you pack. You'd better figure on staying overnight there. I'll give you a check for a hundred dollars. Cash it in the Village as you leave."

But while Eric was packing, his mother came to his room. He saw in a glance that she was in control now, thinking clearly, making her moves with sureness.

"On second thought, Rick," she said, "let's let everything ride until tomorrow."

"Why?"

"It would be better if he came back because he wanted to; and there's a good chance that he'll come drifting back tonight or tomorrow."

"But, Mom—!" Eric saw the long weekend of sun and water slipping from him.

"No buts. We'll give him till noon tomorrow. If he isn't back by then, you can go get him."

Eric awoke every few hours that night listening to cars pass on the road. But none had the sharp, clean bark of the Riley, and each time he would slip back into a light sleep. As a result, he slept soundly until nine o'clock the next morning, when his mother woke him.

About ten he began carrying out camping gear and trying to hang it on the Ossa, one ear tuned to the road.

His mother kept carrying out things she thought he should take—his old Boy Scout canteen, water purification tablets, a snakebite kit.

"Mom, this is a bike, not a truck!"

Behind the saddle he had lashed his sleeping bag, a plump red roll. Extra clothing, twisted into a rope, festooned the handlebars. He tried to maintain an air of gloomy efficiency, the search-and-rescue squad going into action, but the inside of his stomach itched with excitement.

At last he started the engine. His mother raised her hands. "Wait! Heavens! Dad's heart medicine!"

He blipped the throttle while he waited. The engine was tuned to a razor's edge. His father was indeed a mechanic's mechanic. Mrs. Hansen returned with a bottle of tiny white pills.

"If he's sick, call the doctor directly, then call me. He'll fly down."

Then, talking like a boxer's manager, she instructed him to go easy with his father, not to crowd him; to let him know how much they needed him. To build him up; agree with everything he said. It sounded to Eric like playing a fish; he was a bit ashamed of his part in trying to land him, a grown man, like a croaker.

Dutifully he kissed her good-bye and waved to Cruz, who stood in the doorway. He twisted the throttle again and the engine sang out, hot and strong. He felt its power in his bones, and a grin curled one side of his mouth. He tried to stifle it, feeling that it was in bad taste, like a muffled laugh at a funeral. Then he pulled on his helmet.

"Don't worry," he said. "I'll call you."

A wave, a swoop from the parking area. He was on the wing.

chapter **8**

In less than an hour Eric was riding through the steep hills southeast of San Diego. The ridges were high and blue and cattle grazed in narrow valleys. He kept climbing ridges and having to descend into other deep valleys, until at last the road stayed high and turned south. He was approaching the little port of entry of Tecate. On the American side of the line stood a small stucco building. An officer flagged him down and asked for Eric's driver's license.

Eric asked whether a Riley sports car had passed through here Thursday. "It's a Brooklands Nine—my father was driving it. My, uh, grandmother is sick, and—"

"Little green job? Yeah, he went through here. He had a free vaccination, on the house. Said he hadn't had one in three years, and he might as well have it now as when he came out."

"Do you need a vaccination to come back from San Felipe?"

"Sometimes," the officer said mysteriously. "Try us."

Eric hurried over to the phone booth, dropped his change on the floor, recovered it, and reported home. "He was heading for San Felipe, all right!"

His mother said, "Wonderful, darling! Now, be careful on the Rumorosa grade."

Eric said he would, and rode into Mexico with his spirits flying like a flag.

In the town, he bought some of the good Mexican pastry called *pan dulce*. Eating a pink Long Tom, he breezed out east on a ribbon of pavement through high desert country dotted with pines. The air was thin and cool. A half-hour later, beyond a little town, the plateau abruptly collapsed. In a series of benches, it fell thousands of feet to a lion-colored desert speckled with sage; dry watercourses cracked the earth like wrinkles in a hide.

With a high, heady feeling, he swept down through hairpin turns, one after the other, toward a highway that ran like a pencil line toward the big desert city of Mexicali.

In midafternoon he passed through Mexicali's crowded shopping districts and jumbled residential areas. He bought gas, thinking that now he could barely beat the dark to San Felipe. He skimmed on south. Slaglike moon-hills loomed on his right; the sand dunes on his left were frosted with rosy-pink sand verbena. It was unexpectedly beautiful; but in weeks, he knew, the desert heat would burn the flowers to ash.

Now and then, a blue slot on the east, the Gulf of California gleamed. The sun, a flattened orange, began nestling into the sharp-edged hills to the west. He poured on more speed.

The sky was stained with a winy light when he came down a slope and saw San Felipe ahead of him, a ramshackle fishing village on a large bay, offering American tourists motels, trailer camps, stores, and a fish cannery for their catches. He rode through the village to a mole of earth behind the beach. The cool Gulf breeze made his eyes water.

The bay was a depressing brown mud flat drained by the fantastic twenty-foot tide of the upper Gulf. Shrimpers and fishing boats lay askew in the mud, awaiting the next high tide. Steel-blue water shimmered a quarter-mile distant. To the north rose a lank point of land; to the south lay more sand and the motel section. Beached boats were being scraped and painted. Fishermen plodded home through the sand, pants rolled to their knees.

A coolness in the breeze made him suddenly shiver. Night was flooding the land like a tide. He decided to look for the Riley in the motel parking lots first, then work north through the village to the point if necessary. Hurry, hurry! the dying day urged.

But the motel parking lots revealed no green sports car. Of course, he recalled, his father had taken camping gear, and the best campsites were north of town. Passing through the village, he gazed up and down the rutted cross streets. Nothing. North of the village, clots of campers and trailers marred the clean beach, Americans in golf caps and windbreakers drinking beer in camp chairs beside them. But no Riley.

He roared on to the point, the wind cold in his face. Sky and earth had begun to close like a book. In the dusk he rode the length of the point: it was deserted. He chewed a fingernail. Perplexed, he returned to the village and hunted up a small café. Waiting for service, he made triangular traps out of toothpicks and set them off. His father *had* to be here: a sports car could not be driven any farther south, since the pavement ended here, and for seven hundred miles, nearly to the tip of that long, skinny alligator-shape of land called Baja, there was hardly another mile of pavement. The dirt road wandering south from here had the bad reputation of a very tough section of a big city: no one went down it alone.

But if his father had come here, where was he?

The waitress arrived, a pregnant young woman who moved slowly and spoke with the Baja drawl. Eric said he would like some tacos.

"Chicken, beef, or turtle?"

"Two beef, two turtle."

When the woman brought the food, he asked whether a red-headed American had been here recently. She smiled and raised one hand above her head. "Very tall?"

"That's him! With a little green car—"

"Eso! Your father? You're like two beans in a pod."

"When was he here?"

"Yesterday. Ah! See what he did for us . . ." The waitress switched on an electric fan resting on a refrigerator; solemnly it began turning its face this way and that. "It's been broken for months! Your father fixed it. A little wire was burned out—"

"He's pretty handy," Eric agreed. "How, uh—how did he seem? Happy?"

"Very happy. Why not?"

"I just wondered. And he wasn't sick?"

"No. Not sick."

"Because he has a little heart condition—"

"Pobrecito!" exclaimed the waitress. Bad news was so rooted in Mexican life that the mention of serious illness was like a lodge button to establish a relationship. "I'll ask the cook if he knows anything about him," the woman said.

Eric ate. A small boy emerged from the kitchen, shyly looked at him, and scurried outside. In a few minutes he returned and trotted back into the kitchen. Stuffed with tacos, Eric shook a toothpick from an empty tabasco sauce bottle. The waitress came from the kitchen.

"What a pity! They say he left yesterday."

"In which direction?"

"North is the only direction, unless you have a truck or a heep."

Heep? Mexican for "jeep," Eric decided. Discouragement fell on him like a net. Since there was only one way out of the San Felipe bag, his father could now be in Mexicali, the States, anywhere.

His smallest bill was five dollars, and the restaurant could not change it. Eric said he would eat here in the morning and get his change then. When he went out, night had closed on the desert. The sky was like black velvet. The few naked street lights looked lonely, standing in the dirt with dust motes sparkling about them. He wondered where to find a telephone. He had promised to call, and besides he felt a need to touch base with home.

He found a telephone by following a line of poles to a motel. Getting through to San Diego took twenty minutes. There were Morse-codelike beeps, ghostly conversations only half audible, a steady rhythmic humming. Then his mother's voice came in:

"Eric? What did you find out?"

"Well, he was here, but he's gone on."

"But the road ends there, doesn't it?"

"The pavement does. I guess he could have kept going down the trail until he broke the crankcase on a rock, though. Or he might have headed back to Mexicali."

"Oh, fine," his mother said, with a trace of bitterness. "How are you going to find out?"

"Some people are going to ask around for me. I'll check with them in the morning. Somebody must have seen him leave."

"Did they say how he was?"

"The waitress said he seemed fine."

"Thank heaven. Listen, Rick, go to a nice motel and get yourself a room. And don't drink the water."

"Mom, I thought I'd camp out. There's a good beach—"

"Absolutely not. Don't you remember those two boys . . . ?"

"Mom, that was five years ago!" Two boys sleeping in the brush had been bitten by a rabid coyote.

"It could happen again."

"Okay," he said. He had been looking forward to sleeping on the beach. He got a room, rolled his motorcycle inside to be sure it was safe, and, after crawling in bed, ate another *pan dulce*. It was frosted with blue sugar and made him think of the sky. It would have been good to sleep in the open and watch the stars wheel up. But his mother was probably right. This was safer and more comfortable. It just wasn't much fun.

chapter **9**

In the morning, the sea had magically flooded the bay with gray-blue water right up to the beach. Eric stood in his shorts on the motel porch. Stubby, hoydenish shrimp boats were dropping anchor after a night of seining. The things they must bring up in their nets at night! he thought, scratching his chest. Luminous fish, seahorses, plumed snails, and golden *garopas*. He strained to pierce the cool sunlight for a glimpse of the mainland shore, but guessed it was too far to see.

He dressed, then rolled the Ossa from the room. Unsure what to do with his room key, he turned it in at the office. As

an afterthought, he got a twenty changed into Mexican money
in case the café was still short of change.

They were waiting for him at the restaurant. The cook
joined the waitress in relating the news.

"*Ah, mire!*" said the cook, an amiable man with a ruddy
brown face and curly gray hair. "Your father bought a gas can
and a frying pan at a store. Also some cans of food. A fisherman had told him they're catching cabrilla at Puertecitos. He
bought gas at the Pemex station and asked directions."

Eric rubbed his hands together in delight. "Ah-ha! How far
is Puertecitos?"

"Ninety kilometers," said the cook. "Very ugly road, *muy
bronco.*"

Eric calculated: Multiply by six, point off one: fifty-four
miles. On the bike, he could ride there in two hours over the
worst kind of road.

"Many thanks," he said. "I'll have *huevos rancheros,* ham,
toast, and papaya."

Eating, he debated whether to buy a gas can. But there was
nowhere to stow it, and besides he got fifty miles to the gallon
and could buy more gas at Puertecitos. Cabrilla was an in-
shore fish, so probably he could track his father down early,
on the beach, and skin-dive while he surf cast.

He decided to tip big for all this information and left thir-
teen pesos, a dollar. He spent a half-hour buying cans of refried beans, peanut butter, oleo, a small blue pan, and a dozen
of the good hard rolls with the meaty flesh that would keep for
a week. He stuffed them inside his sleeping bag. Then, prodded
by a sense of duty, he again telephoned and told his mother
the latest.

She was relieved, then irritated.

"Isn't that fine? *He* goes fishing while *we* go out of our minds. Tell him—no, what's the use? When he gets tired of fishing, steer him home. Call me from Puertecitos if they have a telephone. All right, dear, you're doing wonderfully. Cut him off at the pass." She gave a wry laugh.

The road south disintegrated in five minutes. He had never seen anything like it. Some long-forgotten rain had turned it to mud, and churning truck wheels had done the rest. It looked as though it had been deep-plowed lengthwise, then fired in an oven. Rocks and scraps of brush had been plugged into the ruts at points where a truck had sunk to the axles in the wet season. Eric rode along the edge, among wildflowers, cactus, and rocks, and managed somehow to keep going. But it was plain that he was not going to average twenty-five miles an hour.

After a half-hour, everything he had tied on had become so loose that he had to pull over and repack. He cut a finger on a sharp bolt and sucked blood from it, worried about infection. Packing, he grew angry at his lumpish lack of dexterity. He kicked a bike wheel, and started over.

A stake-body truck with a load of big sea turtles came lurching along, heading north. Eric flagged it down. "Do you have a little piece of rope?" he asked the driver.

The driver gave him a scrap of cord. He watched Eric fumble with his gear. Finally Eric glanced up, helplessly. The man took the cord from him, as Eric had hoped. With Mexican ingenuity, he hung everything securely on the motorcycle.

"Okay?" he said, standing back.

"Thanks a lot. Can I . . . ?"

The truck driver waved aside the pesos he offered.

The road improved for a while, two deep ruts padded with sand. Standing on the pegs, he rode the Ossa like a cowhorse, letting it bound and squirm under him. Again the Gulf was out of sight. The air heated; he removed his windbreaker and tied the sleeves around his neck.

There were no road signs, and he had little idea how far he had come. He had forgotten to check his odometer. The road climbed some volcanic hills and wound back down to the sea. Beside the ruts there was dim lettering on a cow's skull: *Puertecitos 1 km.* He roared on, came over a rise, and there it was, a hillside colony of house trailers, a few shacky buildings, and a gas pump. The community was wrapped around a small cove. Black volcanic rocks and some kind of dark algae gave the surf an oozy, forbidding look. The Americans sitting by their trailers and campers also looked uninviting. The women were in mail-order sunsuits, the men, golf-capped, all in wash-and-wear pants and shirts. They sat holding their beer cans and gazing at him slack-jawed, like some kind of early man, he thought.

A man in a dirty yachting cap wandered out to the gas pump. The pump was an old lever-type with a glass reservoir that looked as though it might once have held rusty water.

"No gasoline today," said the man.

"That's okay. I'm looking for my father. He's driving a little green sports car. He's tall, has red hair—"

"*Sí, sí, sí.* He camped here one night. He was sick for a little while but he left yesterday."

Eric felt a cold draft. "Sick?"

"*Las tripas.* Just a bellyache."

Eric had heard that a heart attack sometimes disguised itself as indigestion. "Was he all right when he left?" he asked, anxiously.

"Sure. I guess."

"Which way did he go?"

"South. I told him he couldn't make it. The road is steep and very bad."

"Where was he going?"

"To Isla Gaviota. Someone told him about the wonderful fishing there."

Eric slumped. It was turning into a paper chase, or like losing one's hat on a windy day.

"Where's Isla Gaviota?"

"Go south to Goat Point. One of the shark fishermen there will take you out in his boat. I told him he couldn't make it, but he just said, *'Nos tiramos al fondo!'* and drove off laughing."

"Here goes nothing." Very comical. It was only his life he was risking.

"How far is it?" Eric asked.

"Stay on the main road for fifty kilometers. Look for a burned truck body on the right. About a kilometer beyond is the turnoff to the camp."

Eric rode away, not laughing.

Shortly after he left, the road tipped steeply up over some hills. Its surface loosened with rocks and shale. Slewing and spitting pebbles, the Ossa mustanged up the grade. Grease scarred the big rocks in mid-road, where crankcases had dragged over them. How could the Riley possibly have climbed this grade?

Mile by mile the road crumbled away. It turned over on its side as if to shake itself free of any lingering traffic. It stood on end and climbed like a ladder. Eric was worn down with the strain of standing on the pegs while the Ossa bucked under him. Exhausted, he stopped and ate a roll smeared with peanut butter. Then he lay on his back on a boulder and watched buzzards sail like black kites against the sky. The warm sun made him sleepy.

Guiltily he roused himself. No time to waste. Father dying,

son takes nap by road. It was two o'clock and he could not believe he had achieved so little mileage in so many hours.

At last he passed a burned truck body. But it lay in a barranca on the left, not on the right. A cross decorated with faded paper flowers had been propped beside the road: someone had been killed in the wreck, or maybe he had simply given up. Could you die of discouragement? he wondered.

A mile ticked off; another; still another. No side road. Judas Priest! He *did* say a kilometer beyond, didn't he?

Then he passed another truck body, this one on the right. It lay overturned in a wash choked with boulders and cactus; a cluster of three crosses marked it. Many candles had been burned here; the wax glistened on the rocks.

About two kilometers beyond, a mean little detour snaked seaward in serpentine kinks. A wedge of blue gleamed between two hills. With a sense of finality, of knowing the search was ending, he started down this hair-raising drop through brush tangles and boulders. *Got you!* he thought grimly.

Wrestling the bike through a turn near the bottom, he felt a puff of cool air and smelled fish. He breathed deeply. Then a rock turned his front wheel, almost tearing the grips from his fingers. For an instant he was so busy fighting for control— *screech! whump! screech!*—that he came completely in surprise upon a small car headed toward him in the middle of the road.

It was green and angular, and in a glance he knew it was the Riley. A second look told him that the driver was a Mexican, not his father.

He fought the Ossa to a halt. The Riley appeared to be stalled. The driver gazed at him through the dusty windshield. Then he stood up. He was brown and shirtless, with a handkerchief tied about his throat and a crumpled red baseball cap on his head.

chapter **10**

The Mexican climbed out of the car and stood beside it. He wore sandals and floppy gray work pants. With a stubble of black whiskers on his face, he looked tough and sinister. Eric licked his dry lips. He pressed the kill switch and the engine coughed and expired.

"I, uh, I'm looking for my father," he said, in Spanish. "I think that's his car."

"No American here," said the Mexican firmly.

"No, I mean in the fish camp. Isn't there a camp at the beach?"

"*Sí*. But no American there. I just came from there."

"Well, uh." Eric knew he was handling this badly. But what could he do? "That's his car, isn't it?" he said.

The man shook his head. "My car."

"Have you got the registration slip on it?" Eric asked. He got off the Ossa and went toward him, his heart thudding. He would try to keep him talking until he thought of a clincher of some kind, or the man attacked him. The man looked fast and hard as a panther.

"Are you a fisherman?" he asked.

The red baseball cap nodded. Relaxing, the Mexican leaned against the fender. He took out a pack of cigarettes and offered Eric one. When Eric shook his head, he replaced them in his pants pocket. His face, thin and brown, looked as though it had been cured in brine.

"Sure—I fish and spear turtles. I am a *vagabundo del mar.*"

A vagabond of the sea. Kind of like a tramp, Eric guessed. A sea gypsy. "Oh," he said.

"A free life. I own nothing but my *panga* and all the fish in the Gulf of California."

"Panga?" Eric said.

Holding his hands apart as though making a cat's cradle, the fisherman said:

"My—you understand—my boat, my outfit."

"What about your car?" asked Eric.

Removing the wet cigarette from his lips, the man frowned at it. "Now, that is what worries me. Did I make a mistake? I traded my *panga* to an American for his car."

Shocked, Eric gulped: "But you said—"

"It's true, he's not here! He's sailed to Isla Gaviota." A bird sailed above them and he pointed upward with a look of happy discovery. *"Gaviota!* 'Siggle' in English, no? Seegle?"

"Sea gull," Eric said. "Sea gull."

"Sea. Gall. Thank you."

Eric squatted and picked up a little stick, with which he made a couple of marks in the earth. Since it was the universal thinking posture, the *vagabundo* squatted beside him, found another stick, and also made marks.

"You traded just for the day, eh?" said Eric.

"No. Final. Finish! He's a *vagabundo,* now." The man laughed.

The stick broke in Eric's fingers. Using the stub, frowning, he made another mark on the stony earth.

"How much is a *panga* worth?" he asked.

"How much is anything worth? How much is a wife worth when you see her every day? Not much. But how much is she worth when you come back from four months at sea?"

He poked Eric with his stick and laughed. Eric grinned waxily.

"The car is worth about, oh, four thousand dollars," he said.

"Chihuahua!" whispered the Mexican. "What have I done?"

"How much is your *panga* worth?"

"Two hundred dollars for a Topolobampo boat like mine. Another twenty-thirty dollars for the gear. Harpoon. Machete."

"So you'll have to trade it back to him," said Eric firmly. He had the mystery all nailed down, now. His father had gotten drunk and traded outfits. The Mexican, for Mexicans were very honorable people away from the lurid border towns, now realized he had cheated him badly. He was remorseful.

"We'll find him and get your boat back," he said.

But the man said, "No—finish! But what am I going to do with four thousand dollars? Get so drunk I . . ." He made a grimace of disgust. He touched his chin to indicate dribble. "And after a week or two I have nothing left, nothing."

"Then you'd better trade back!"

"He's gone. I don't think he'd trade anyway. It is a beautiful boat, yellow and smooth as a banana."

"When did he leave?"

"Yesterday."

"To fish?"

"And to explore the island, he said. There is a great treasure buried there, millions of pesos! You see, when the Jesuits were driven from the missions—" and he related the hoary old tale of the Jesuit fathers burying the gold and silver they had held out on the King of Spain. Nobody so far had found so much as a seventeenth-century bottle cap at any of the old missions in Baja.

Eric realized he was stalled for the moment. The *vagabundo* had no intention of parting with the Riley, even considering it as a health hazard. It was final, finish, ended, as far as he was concerned.

Making a last scratch in the earth, Eric stood up. "Can somebody in the village tell me how to get to the island?"

"Talk to Gregorio, the old man there. He's dressing a shark at the south end of the camp. He's got a boat with a motor and he might take you. *Ah, míre!* Maybe you'll kindly get my car started again for me."

Eric thought of stealing the keys or taking out the distributor rotor. He decided there was a greater chance of getting caught than there was of the Mexican's getting far. So he got in, sniffed the odor of gas, and finding the choke pulled all the way out explained about flooding the carburetor. He held the accelerator down until the cylinders aired out, then started it. The Mexican was so delighted when he got out that he clasped

Eric in the classical Latin *abrazo*. Eric was pleased, though still in mild shock.

"It's all set," he said. "For Pete's sake, take it easy going over the rocks!"

Five minutes later, the trail wandered from a thicket onto a beach. A sharp little cove was cut into the reddish volcanic hills. He saw green water edged by a thin lace of surf; three stark-looking pink islands rose a few miles offshore.

A few hundred yards south he saw the fish camp. It was not a town, not even a village, merely a *población,* a place with a few inhabitants. Huts were scattered along a narrow strip between beach and foothills. Eric rode down the hard white beach of crushed shell into a ramshackle sprawl of reed fences, lean-tos, and cactus corrals. On the beach knelt some small children cleaning fish. Here and there he saw strings of fish meat drying on lines.

At the far end of the camp a dugout canoe lay overturned on the sand. It had pale-blue sides and a bottom of indigo blue. A man was caulking it. Near the boat stood the last hut in the camp, a somewhat better-looking one with a thatched roof and walls of palm fans. A rusty gasoline barrel rested on a trestle near the door. In the shade of a simple pole-and-thatch shelter an old man was dressing a hammerhead shark. Near him was a line of drying fish, some of the meat pink, some dry and gray. A basket of dried shark fins, like gray cards, baked in the sun. A gang of buzzards were gorging themselves on the carcass of another shark nearby.

The old man glanced up as Eric parked the Ossa. He wore little more than rags and sandals, but looked brown and healthy. " *'Tardes,*" said Eric.

" *'Tardes,*" said the old man. He gave his knife a quick whet on a stone and resumed slicing meat.

"Are you Gregorio?" Eric brushed a fly from his face.

"At your service."

"Much pleasure," Eric said, extending his hand. "I'm Eric Hansen, Junior. I'm looking for my father, Eric Hansen, *Senior*."

They shook hands. Eric told him what the *vagabundo* had said about his father's trading his car for a boat. As he talked he got a good look at Gregorio's face. It was very brown and wrinkled, and he had a ruined eye that resembled a discolored ball of salt. When he spoke, he displayed a set of fine false teeth, so manufactured-looking that it seemed as though he might have to wind them up to eat.

"So I've got to get out to the island and find him," Eric finished. Another fly settled on his ear and he slapped at it.

"Why?" asked Gregorio. "He's a man, isn't he, *joven?* Leave him alone."

Clearly, Eric saw, he was up against some primitive dominant-male philosophy. He knew that in Mexico a husband was a king; his behavior was not to be questioned by his family. In the abstract, the idea had appeal. But he was here to find his father before he died, or gave away everything he had and starved on some naked stone island drenched by the sea.

While he hesitated, Gregorio waved the knife at a white boat resting on the sand far from the water. "He fixed my motor so it would run!" he said. "It's never run so well since the first week I owned it."

"He's great with machinery," Eric said. "He even invented a pair of pliers once."

Gregorio reached in his pocket and displayed a gleaming new pair of HanDeeRench pliers. "He gave me a pair. *Muy buen hombre.* What do you want him for?"

"Well, he—he's got a family. We need him."

"You're poor people?"

"No, no. But he's the man of the family. And—"

"Aha! The man!" Gregorio said, holding the knife vertically. "It's what I was trying to say."

"Anyway, he's sick." Eric suddenly dug out the little plastic bottle of pills. "His heart! If he strained himself, he might die."

Gregorio clucked sympathetically. "I'll tell you what. In the morning I'll take you out to the island. Today I have this fish to finish with, and anyway it will be dark in a couple of hours and there isn't time."

"I'll pay you," Eric said in desperation. "Ten dollars—fifteen! Can't we go now?"

The old man scowled. "I have this shark to finish. Talk to that fellow caulking his boat. He's another stranger, just came in today. Maybe he'll sell you his boat."

"I don't want to buy one, just rent one."

"Well, nobody else here has a motor, and it's two or three hours by canoe."

Depressed, Eric gazed at the man kneeling on the hull of the overturned boat tapping caulking material into a crack. "Is that another voyager, or whatever you call them?"

"Vagabundo, not voyager. It's a totally different thing. A voyager is going somewhere. A *vagabundo* is already there. It's his way of life, gypsying up and down the Gulf."

"Huh," Eric said.

"He fishes to live, and lives to fish. When he needs a little money, he spears a turtle or two to sell in some town. Or a big queen shell, or a trash-pearl, something like that. Americans buy them in La Paz. I was a *vagabundo* for twenty years. Where I hit shore, that was my home. But an old man needs a roof and a wife, so I stopped here and married a seventeen-year-old girl when I was fifty."

"Mmm," said Eric. He peered at the trio of distant islands lying on the pale blue water like oystershells. Already their bare sides were tinged with sunset color. "Which one of those is Isla Gaviota?"

"The big one in the middle. You'd better talk to that *vagabundo* there. Because I'll tell you the truth, boy, I don't think El Rojo is coming back. I think he'll head right on down the coast. Freedom is like a fever, or love. When you haven't had it before, it sweeps you off your feet."

"El Rojo?"

"Your father. 'The Redhead,' we called him."

"What did he say he was going to do?" Eric pleaded.

"He said, *'Nos tiramos al fondo!'* And away he went!"

Here goes nothing. "Oh, man," Eric muttered. It was not El Rojo he was following, it was El Loco.

Kneeling, he bent into a hump of indecision, watching Gregorio strip off shark meat and hang it on the line in translucent pink rags. The buzzards greedily dipped their heads into the abdomen of the carcass on the beach and plucked out nauseating tidbits. *Thump, thump, thump* went the stick the fisherman was using as a caulking mallet.

This was a real bind; the worst. He should call his mother, but the nearest telephone was back at San Felipe. If he rode back, El Rojo might get a lead on him he would never overcome. He had to bag him while he was still on the island; bring him to his senses somehow. Trading his car for a beat-up dugout canoe! He was sick, all right.

He wandered across the beach toward the dugout. On the sand were dozens of shark jaws and twisted, leathery carcasses. He stopped near the overturned boat, his hands shoved deep in his pockets as though searching for lost raisins. The *vagabundo* appeared to be about forty-five, with dusty black hair, black whisker stubble, and thin brown skin pulled unevenly over the cheekbones in fine wrinkles, like the paper on a model airplane. A fly crawled over his face, but he appeared not to feel it. His pants were rolled to the knees. He looked at Eric and smiled.

"Hello," he said.

The boat had a deep canoe shape, with the rounded curves of a woman's breast. The hull was smooth and well painted. A roll of poles and canvas lay on the sand. The man was dipping bits of string and cow hair in paint and tapping them into a fine crack with a screwdriver.

"Will your boat carry two people?" Eric asked.

"Why not?"

"I'll pay you ten dollars to take me out to Isla Gaviota tonight."

"Tomorrow. The caulking must dry."

"Tomorrow will be too late."

The *vagabundo* shrugged.

"Tomorrow I can get Gregorio to take me," Eric said.

"That's good. What's your name?"

"Eric Hansen."

"I thought so. Your father is a fine fellow. I'm Angel Verdugo."

"Much pleasure. He's going to get in trouble, though, the way he's going."

"Borracho?"

"No, he doesn't drink much. But he's sick. And I think he must be out of his mind. He traded his car for a canoe!"

Looking up in surprise, Angel said, "But you can't drive a car to an island, boy! It was the only thing to do."

"No! You see . . . well, look . . ." Eric massaged the

back of his neck with both hands. These people reasoned like mountain goats. They had a primitive sort of logic that mocked common sense.

"If you want to follow him," said Angel, "I'll trade you my *panga* for your motorcycle."

"No! Out of the question."

"Throw in everything," cried the Mexican, indicating with a wave his water bottles, oars, hand lines, and harpoon. There were also a blanket, some cooking pots, and a dirty cloth sack of food.

"Forget it! Final! Finish!" Eric mumbled good-bye and walked off.

chapter **11**

Out in the tranquil water of the cove, big mullet were jump-
ing. Eric guessed there was about an hour of daylight left. He
rode down the beach, away from the fish camp with its flies,
and found a good campsite beside an elephant tree. It was a
weird, squat tree with a gray bulbous trunk and a modest head
of small leaves.

He checked his gasoline; he had only two gallons left. That
would barely get him back to San Felipe. Unpacking, he
spread his sleeping bag on a small tarp and beat the dust from
it. He collected firewood and made a ring of red stones. He

was hungry. He gazed at the water, speculatively, as a food source. He had speared a cabrilla on an overnight trip to San Felipe two years ago; they all agreed it was the best fish they had ever eaten. He decided to try for one.

He pulled on his trunks and cocked his Tommy gun-like spear gun. In swim fins and face mask, he waded into the water. It was as warm and still as bathwater, so clear that resting on the bottom he felt like a specimen preserved in a block of plastic. Schools of yellow and black angelfish rushed by, passing so close that they seemed to go through rather than around him. He smiled at the beauty of the reef. Purple sea urchins with black spines clustered the rocks; pink gorgonia-like fans grew from the bottom. A huge snail with a red body inched majestically along.

Cruising, he kept taking deep, tension-releasing sighs. *Great, great!* he said to himself. A beautiful golden fish cruised past but he lacked the heart to spear it. A moment later he saw a chunky green fish with white stars sprinkled over its body: a cabrilla!

Thumbing the gun off safety, he began stalking it. The fish raced ahead, then cut back. *Thunk!* the gun kicked and the spear flashed away. The fish limply struggled. Eric pulled in the nylon cord and swam to shore with the fish still on the spear. He felt the man-pride of a frontiersman.

Made camp at sundown and shot me a cabrilla for supper. E. Hansen.

But his woodcraft broke down when it came to cleaning the fish. He had always left that to his mother or to Cruz. He butchered it hopelessly, and soon had guts, half-digested weeds, and blood all over his hands. Disgusted, he carried the fish to the edge of the water and washed it off. Then he laid it on a rock and hacked off some irregular pieces of pink flesh, muttering to himself. He knew there was a way to get neat little filets without bone or scale. But this was not the way.

While he got a fire going, flies swarmed on the fish until he covered it with a pan. Then he melted some oleo and put the fish and one of his cans of refried beans to heat. With the fragrance of cooking food, his spirits rose. Night was flowing over the volcanic hills behind him. He could see fires and lamps in the fish camp, warm yellow morsels of civilization.

He ate from his Boy Scout mess kit, grinning to himself. But, suddenly, guilt crawled over him like a caterpillar. He thought of his father living it up so foolishly out on Isla Gaviota; of himself enjoying all this as though it were a camping trip.

Pretty rough on Mom, he thought. A few minutes later, however, he lay back, stuffed, and smiled drunkenly at the lights of a shrimp boat plowing past on its way to the shrimp beds. A cold breeze came up.

And now it was dark. He stripped to his shorts and crawled into his sleeping bag. The little waves bumped on the shore. He dozed and woke again. The sky was now wonderfully black, the stars crisp and white. It was cool and breezy outside, but in his bedroll he was warm, and felt sorry for people in houses.

Several times that night he awoke thinking he had merely dozed off; but each time the stars had wheeled up higher. It gave him a sense of being part of some vaster and slower system than he had ever imagined, simple yet inexplicable, as though he were a very small part but one that, like a nut or bolt or an idler wheel, performed a job no other part of the machine could. Living like this, he thought, a man could become a star- or space-worshiper. He was lying on the earth and it was turning under him! Never before had he been quite convinced that it really happened.

Daylight came tugging at him like a puppy. He drew his head into the sleeping bag and hoped it would go away. But the light pierced his eyelids and he raised his head groggily and gazed around. His diving watch said 6:15. Everything was washed with a rosy light. Overhead a flock of tiny pink clouds grazed like lambs toward the sun. In the brush, birds were shyly tuning up. A woodpecker hammered on a tree.

He sat up for a while, blinking. His hip remembered a stone he had lain on. Gradually he came to and tried to think of breakfast. He had no coffee, no milk, no eggs, no cereal. Glumly he made a second entry in his journal.

This day I had me no breakfast. E. Hansen.

As he was building a fire, a boy ran up and pushed a little parcel at him. He spoke through his nose in such backwoods Spanish that Eric could hardly make sense of it.

"My uncle said to give you this."

"Thanks!"

In the package were an egg and four corn tortillas. Pleased, Eric boiled the egg and reheated last night's beans. He laid the tortillas on the beans to heat with them. Cross-legged, he sat down to eat, noticing with relief that the flies had not come on duty yet.

Afterward, he brushed his teeth and washed his dishes in the surf. Walking up the beach, he passed the *vagabundo,* who wore a knitted black watch cap and a grin.

"I'll tell you what," said the man. "I'll spend a couple of hours showing you how to sail the boat and catch shark."

"No, thanks," Eric said.

By his crooked *jacal,* Gregorio was cleaning his false teeth in a basin. He rinsed his mouth and rubbed his gums. "Very good teeth," he said, "but they hurt me a little. The dentist will be by again some day and fix them."

"A dentist really comes here?"

"Dr. Nestor, an American. He has a little truck with big tires, and he gets around, believe me. From one end of Baja to the other. And his daughter—you should see her! Tall—an Amazon. And hair like gold. Well, about today. . ."

He said he could not afford to make the trip without combining it with business, so Eric would have to help him on the fishing. While they cruised to Isla Gaviota, Eric could bait hooks. They would set the ground line, then hunt for his father.

Eric felt time bleeding away, yet knew it would have to be Gregorio's way or not at all.

With Gregorio carrying a gunnysack of bait, Eric a can of gasoline, they waded out to the boat, floating now in two feet of crystal water. With a roar and a burst of blue smoke, the motor ignited.

In an hour they reached Conejo, the southernmost of the three stark islands. These were the old man's fishing waters. Using a small, sharp machete, Eric chopped the bait fish in two and hooked a piece on each of the hooks, of which there were dozens. The hooks were fastened to six-foot lengths of cord, in turn fixed to a long groundline that would be anchored to the bottom. Gregorio lowered an anchor, then tied on a large glass float, bottle-green in a snood of woven rope. A white flag was thrust into the snood to help locate the float later.

They cruised on, Eric paying out line and hooks. At the far end of the rope, they dropped a second anchor and rigged another float and flag.

"Okay!" said the old man gaily. "Now we look for El Rojo."

He tossed out a baited hand line for food fish, then headed north along the sheltered side of the island. Eric saw no possibility of a boat's being beached anywhere. The rocky cliffs plunged straight into the water. Big *cardón* cactus clung to the cliffs, pipe-organlike plants taller than many trees. In a geyser of spray, a cruising pelican suddenly fell into the sea with all the grace of a suicide leaping from a bridge.

At the north end of the island, Gregorio shouted, "We'd better look over the other island while we're here!"

But the only beach on the northernmost island was deserted. They cruised down the weather side of Gaviota, seeing several small beaches, all of them deserted. At last they came to a beach where a crude pole shelter stood under a red cliff. Though there was no sign of a boat, the shark fisherman headed in anyway, cutting power in the shallows.

"Time to eat!" he explained.

Eric groaned. Time, time!

"Can't we eat as we go?" he pleaded.

"Ha, ha! You like raw fish, boy?" Gregorio held up a red snapper he had pulled in during the run.

Eric blew out his cheeks in resignation and climbed from the boat. As they beached the craft, Gregorio noticed something: yellow paint on a rock in the water.

"Aha! This is where he beached his boat, the rascal!"

Eric inspected the shelter. Someone had spent the night there. A long indentation revealed where a sleeping bag had lain. Empty cans, unrusted, lay in a fire ring. Gregorio thrust his hand into the ashes, then shook his head.

"Bad luck, *joven*. He left here yesterday."

"Hell," Eric said bitterly.

Gregorio put one finger to the tip of his nose. "On the other hand, he may have passed *last* night on Conejo. Maybe he's still there."

Eric rubbed the back of his neck. "Gregorio, if we don't

find him, I've got to get word to my mother. It's urgent. Where can I telephone?"

"There is a telephone at Puertecitos; but if he's heading south you don't want to go north. I have it! A day or two down the coast there's a place called Bahía San Jorge. Shrimp boats anchor there. One of them would send a message to a radio operator in San Diego, who would telephone your mother."

Eric kicked some sand. Or how about a carrier pigeon? he thought. "Okay. Let's eat and then hit Conejo."

"Fine! It's settled!"

What's he so happy about? Eric thought, grumpily. Nothing was settled except that they were about to eat.

With skill, Gregorio extracted two perfect filets from the red snapper without disturbing the innards. Then he built a fire, cooked the fish, warmed tortillas. They ate; but instead of preparing to take off afterward, the old man lay down and pulled his hat over his face. Eric stood frowning at him. He was as impossible to hurry as a celestial body. A raw nerve in Eric's brain writhed like a sandpapered snake.

To kill time, he wandered along a line of beach-worn shells at the high-tide line, picking up the interesting ones. They were nearly all new to him, and soon his pockets were full. Then, finding even better shells, he emptied his pockets and started over. Lulled by the whisper of little waves, the tangy breeze on his cheek, he yawned. The small nerve in his brain lay still.

He settled himself on the sand, face down, his head resting on his arms, and fell asleep.

Much later—the sun was behind the island—a hand patted his shoulder. He looked up. "Huh? What?"

Gregorio said, "*Vámonos!*"

They launched the boat and hedge-hopped down the island to Isla Conejo. But that island, too, was deserted. The old man came up and sat on the thwart beside Eric.

"Well, now what? He's gone south."

"I'll pay you twenty dollars to take me to Bahía San Jorge tomorrow! He can't be any farther than that. Or could I make it on my motorcycle?"

"The road does not go directly to San Luis. It goes inland for fifty miles—a day's travel. No, I'm sorry. Tomorrow I take in my catch."

"Thirty dollars?" Eric said.

"It's too far to go in this boat. I couldn't even carry enough gasoline. Besides, it would be hard on the motor. In a *panga* like your father's, you can set sail and travel like a bird."

Gloomily, Eric reviewed his options.

Option One: to go home.

Option Two: to return to Puertecitos and telephone for instructions.

Option Three: to buy the blue panga and follow, before El Rojo got completely out of range.

Gregorio stepped up the motor. They hurried landward, bow wave sloshing. Eric's mouth drew sulkily as he pondered, anticipating his mother's comments; whatever he did, it would be wrong: he should have *made* Gregorio take him out yesterday; he shouldn't have backtracked to Puertecitos and let his father get so far ahead.

"Surely, dear, so close, you could have thought of *something* . . ." she would say.

At low tide, they floated in and dropped anchor. They carried gear to the shack. Eric had no idea what to do next. Go home, he guessed. Give up. Yet his mind balked at the idea of returning while his father was still recklessly plunging on. He was sick, mentally if not physically. But though he knew he must go on, there was no practical way to continue.

He got out his money to pay Gregorio.

"No charge," said the old man. "You fished."

But Eric made him take fifty pesos. Gregorio went into the shack and brought out two cans of beer. *"Un traguito?"* he said.

Eric hesitated. "Okay."

Though not cold, the beer tasted better than beers he had sneaked at home. Soon a warm little buzzing commenced in his head. The whining brain nerve fell asleep like a sick child. Finishing his beer, Eric said,

"That was good, old-timer. Thanks a lot."

"Have another?"

Eric crushed the can and hurled it at a rock, missing it by a yard. "Well, I might," he said.

With the second beer, wisdom surfaced through the tangled seaweed of his doubts and anxieties. He saw with clarity what must be done. He shed his worries like a snakeskin.

In no hurry to act, he chatted with Gregorio as the shadows lengthened. He asked what had happened to his eye, and got the story. "Damn' shark hook," said the old man. He asked where he sold his dried shark meat. And what did he do with the fins?

Gregorio smiled. The meat was sold to a man who came through now and then in a truck. The shark fins went to China for soup. No kidding? No kidding. Was it true, also, that they distilled a liquor down here that made girls passionate? Absolutely! It was sweet and strong, made from a shrub called *damiana,* and you must never drink it on an empty stomach, for it was not only girls who were susceptible to it. Chihuahua!

Eric patted Gregorio on the shoulder. In the dusk he

trudged down the sand to where the *vagabundo,* his boat righted, was loading gear into it.

"What do you say, *amigo?*" Eric greeted him.

The man slapped the boat's stern. "She's all ready for another thousand miles, kid. Look at that anchor! Real lead. I made it myself, in the form of a stingray! Turn it over—there are real stingray grinders in its mouth."

Eric saw that the anchor did indeed resemble a round stingray with a ring in the tail. "How about that?" he chuckled.

"The sails are new," said Angel. "The sailmaker wanted me to take brown canvas because it was cheaper. But the only color for sails is white. In the race in La Paz Bay last year we looked like sea gulls coming down the water. And I won!"

"White is the color of my true love's sails," quoted Eric. Vaguely aware that he was not behaving quite normally, he wondered whether it was noticeable.

The *vagabundo* smiled without comprehension at the joke.

"Okay," Eric said abruptly. "It's a deal. I'd better show you how to operate the bike before dark. I won't have time in the morning."

"And in the morning I'll teach you how the boat works. Though there is little to learn. You simply spread your wings like a bird, and *pronto!* you're flying!"

chapter 12

It was impossible.

He would never have done it.

But there it was: The motorcycle was far up the beach near the blue canoe. Eric had thought, until he saw the Ossa in the dawn, that he had dreamed it. Now he remembered shaking hands on the deal and giving the man a riding lesson.

He sat cross-legged on his sleeping bag while his brain emerged blinking from its cave. Painfully he retraced the steps that had led him to the trade; and in the end he realized there had been nothing else to do. The beer had merely made the decision more palatable.

He simply had to stay on his father's trail until he bagged him. And the only way to travel in a country without roads was by boat.

The fact remained, however, that he was embarking with about eighty dollars in his pocket, on a body of water with a very bad name. Narrow though it was, the Gulf brewed strange, roaring tides and was mined with reefs; its storm troughs were too deep and short to ride like ocean swells. There was no right way to hit them, he had heard.

The roar of the motorcycle brought his head up. Through puffy eyes he saw Angel, shirtless, swerving down the beach toward him. The *vagabundo* pulled up.

"Hop on! The old man has invited us to breakfast."

Gregorio served scrambled eggs and a *machaca* of turtle meat with onions and peppers. He and Angel explained the Gulf to Eric—the mystique of tide, wind, and weather. Both wore religious medals which they claimed had pulled them through many a tight spot. In the end, the technique seemed to be to do this or that, then pray.

Gregorio handed him a stained paper bag.

"Here is food you may need. With luck, you'll be in Bahía San Jorge tomorrow night. There's a store there. Tell your father Gregorio carries the pliers close to his heart!"

They went down to the boat. Beside it, Angel spread the gear that was part of his *panga,* now Eric's. Hand lines to troll with, a harpoon for turtles, a battered bucket. A large machete and a small one. Two cooking pots, a coil of rope, old wine bottles for water. No compass, no charts.

Looking it over, Eric decided there was nothing you couldn't have bought in Sparta three thousand years ago.

The canoe itself was fifteen feet long, dug out of a log and painted blue outside, red inside. It was three feet wide and pointed at both ends. A thwart was wedged into each end and the middle. The mast was stubby and carried a triangular mainsail and a small jib. There were two paddles.

Eric collected his gear and carried it to the boat. They stowed it. Then Gregorio helped them push the heavy canoe into the water. With buyer and seller paddling, they embarked on the test run.

Until the wind picked up, they paddled. Eric was frustrated to discover that every stroke threw the boat off course; the trick, he learned, was to hold the blade in the water after the stroke, as a rudder.

As the wind rose, Angel hoisted sail and threaded the handle of his paddle up through a rope ring at the stern. When he hauled in the mainsheet, the wind took the heavy hull and drove it along. The fisherman demonstrated the trimming of the sails, then had Eric take the tiller.

After yawing around for a while, Eric caught on. A small thrill rose through him like a bubble. He felt that the boat had a life and a mind of its own. It was a question of understanding and cooperating with its whims. Now he understood something he had read about boats.

"Man, building this greatest and most personal of tools, has received a boat-shaped mind, and the boat, a man-shaped soul." Saying it to himself, he shivered.

Angel, watching him, saw this knowledge dawning, and smiled. He turned the boat back.

They shook hands on the beach. Then the helmeted *vagabundo* set off for San Felipe on the motorcycle, and the watch-capped cyclist headed south in the canoe.

chapter **13**

In midafternoon, Eric made out a sail several miles to the south, a mere snowflake on the water. Like a mirage, it kept its distance from him. Then a point of land, long, low, and lizard-shaped, rose in the south. The other boat seemed to be gliding out east to pass the point. Eric adjusted course to stay with it. *Ah-ha!* he thought. *Got you!*

His watch said four o'clock. He had eaten some rolls and peanut butter for lunch, but they had not stayed with him. He thought obsessively of food, of hamburgers and cherry pie, chocolate malts and French fries. What Gregorio had given him were such provisions as dried shark meat, chilis, and three shark fins like gray cardboard. He had no idea how to make anything edible out of them. There were two eggs in the sack, but he was saving them for breakfast. Finally he threaded a strip of bait onto a hook and threw out a hand line.

When he searched for the sail again, he found it silhouetted halfway out on the long, low hulk of the point. The point itself seemed to have slid still farther east. With dismay he saw what had happened: the wind had blown the keelless *panga* far off course; he was slowly being blown ashore. He let the mainsail flap and began paddling. To be so close to his father and then lose him—! In panic he prayed: *Don't let him get away!*

Soon the tender areas on his palms were swelling into plump blisters. With his foot, he snaked a sack of gear to him and found a greasy rag inside it. He wrapped the rag about the paddle and resumed stroking. But with his blisters hurting less, he become conscious of his rump and shoulder muscles being tender.

The hand line, tied to a cleat, began to thrum. He hauled in a pan-sized fish, slim and fast-looking, with orange spots on its sides. After stowing the fish in wet burlap, he searched again for the sail. In alarm, he saw that the tiny flake of white was just sliding out of sight around the point. As he watched, it vanished. He rested a moment, gazing with a pang at the place where he had last seen the sail. Reason argued that if the sail had belonged to a keelless *panga* like his own, it would have been driven off course too. On the other hand, perhaps the sail was merely flapping, and the true motive power was some-one's paddle. The other possibility was that it was a much larger sailboat than it had appeared, cruising easily under full canvas. Yet he clung to the hope that the boatman was El Rojo.

In any event, he saw with a shiver of anxiety that the sun had dropped behind the gaunt hills. Night was stealing upon him like a thief. He must find a sandy place to land, gather firewood, get set for the night. In all his life, he had never been completely alone at night. Last night, at least, there had been a village nearby. He turned toward shore and scurried for safety.

Just before dark he spotted a stretch of sand between the water and the hills. He made a landing and pulled the boat up as far as possible before dropping the anchor on the sand, then gazed up and down the beach. No smoke, no sign of life.

Armed with a machete, he started a hunt for kindling. He found no shrubs with a trunk thicker than his wrist. But what he found was dry, and with it he built a fire near a *cardón,* more for the company of the plant than for shelter, since it had the sparse growth pattern of a telephone pole. Then he hurried down to the boat and got his fish. This time the cleaning went better. He saved some of the waste for bait.

He ate by firelight, the fish delicious, the beans the best, the roll's white heart still soft. Later, standing in six inches of water, he brushed his teeth. He scoured his utensils with sand, rinsed them in salt water, and placed them near the fire.

Gratefully he sought his sleeping bag. He slid his legs into the outing flannel cocoon, wriggled around, stuffed some underwear beneath his head. The breeze was cold and he kept his watch cap on. He listened to the rasp of little waves on the beach. A bird made strange cries. Coyotes yapped and howled. Far out on the Gulf a single light gleamed, a shrimp boat going to work.

The sun rolled him out early. He cooked the rest of the fish and boiled the eggs. Eating, he studied the point. It consisted of a sucession of tawny hills running out to a rocky cliff a couple of miles east. The hills were not very high, and he decided to climb them before he started, to learn whether the other *vagabundo* might have camped across the point.

In twenty minutes he had reached the summit and was gazing down its backslope. A surprisingly strong wind blew in his face. The barren slopes plunged abruptly into the water with only a scrap of beach here and there. The water, clear green in the shallows, sloped into the Gulf in bands of deepening color.

Suddenly he saw a sail. A boat was anchored below him to the right, about a half-mile distant! But in the crisp light, he saw that its hull was red. Two men were wading to it with armloads of gear, and it was obviously larger than a dugout canoe. As he watched, the boat put out and pointed south.

As far as he could see, not another boat was visible. He was disturbed to notice clouds covering the coastal mountains. Out in the Gulf, a haze had begun to smear the sky. Whitecaps popped up and melted away. Angel had cautioned him against the sudden, howling winds of the Gulf. Should he try to make the point, round it, scamper along close to shore? He supposed it was safe; yet he saw few beaches, and there were many rocky islets studding the shoreline.

He decided to round the point, haul down the sail, continue by paddle in shallow water. As he set out, however, he found that the wind had shifted and was dead against him. He furled the sail and started paddling. His sore shoulder muscles ached as he dug the blade into the water. His palms were tender.

Minute by minute the wind strengthened. By the time he reached the tip of the point it was tearing the tops off waves and hurling stinging sheets of water over him. Just off the point stood a small, jagged islet white with birdlime. The waves smashed fretfully against it. With his heart beating faster and an empty feeling at the pit of his stomach, he headed through the passage between the rocks and the islet. In thirty seconds he was caught in a violent current and paddling for his life. Sharp rocks, inches under the surface, mined the passage. He heard a rock thump the hull; cold sweat formed on his face. He clenched the paddle and drove hard for the open water beyond the rocks. The sea took the boat and rocked it. Another rock grazed the bottom. In his ears was the seethe and wash of waves striking the weather side of the point. He wished desperately that there were someone, anyone, to turn the whole thing over to.

He knelt on the floor and paddled savagely. Bubbles gurgled under his knees. Green water broke over the bow, and now there was four inches of water sloshing around in the bilge. He moaned.

At last the rocks were behind him. He continued to paddle frantically, getting sea room before turning back along the south side of the point. Now he was broadside to the waves and rolling dangerously. The wind was stronger still. Heaps of lemonade-colored foam blew about among the rocks. Ahead of him he saw a spit of sand. Gasping, he stroked abreast of it. He started to head in, then remembered Angel's advice to back onto a beach rather than hit it head-on. The waves swept him in stern-first. He grounded heavily.

He scrambled out and got the canoe up on the sand. All the water ran to the bow and he was able to bail with the bucket. Exhausted and slightly sick with the rolling, he spread his wet gear on some shrubs to dry and sat down. He found he was trembling. After he had rested, he gathered his things and set out once more.

All morning he weathered along. He ate rolls and peanut butter again for lunch. His sailing plan was to paddle as long as he could, then keep the boat headed into the weather while he caught his breath. Once, as he let his aching shoulders rest, he caught a fish on the hand line.

By four o'clock, he knew he would have to quit. He was exhausted and half-starved. He saw no smoke, had seen no fishing boats. But now that he was ready to go ashore, the Gulf would not let him: the rocky cliffs stood in the water without a fringe of sand.

The sun poised on the rim of the jagged hills. Misgivings gnawed at him. Due south a mile or so rose a very small, bare island a quarter-mile offshore. Was there a narrow beach on its lee side? He paddled desperately. In a half-hour he was in the passage and it was nearly dark. The sand proved to be merely foam. From the mainland shore, he heard the clatter of cobbles tossed by the surf: a landing there would be impossible. And the island was simply a huge stone. In the windy dusk, pelicans and small sea birds circled its crest, squawking.

Close in, he paddled along, searching for a cove, a beach, any sort of landing. Here, in the lee of the island, the water was calm. Just ahead he saw a dark inlet like the mouth of a hidden river. But the stone cliffs that formed it fell vertically to the water. He hurried on, rounding the lower end of the island in almost complete dark. Panic flew up at him as the sea took the boat again. Shivering, he worked back along the weather side of the island. There was no landing, no shelter.

His mind made up, he circled the north end of the island, paddled back to the inlet, and drove the canoe into the wedge of still water. He lowered the anchor. He was out of the wind and the water was still. He gave a sigh.

For a while he merely sat, sandbagged with fatigue. Then he made a pallet of the sail and tarp and spread his sleeping bag upon it. He ate a can of cold beans, using a tortilla as a fork. He made cold coffee and devoured peanut butter out of the jar. Then he slid into the sleeping bag, gazed slack-jawed up at the sky, and in moments was asleep.

chapter **14**

Inch by inch Eric crawled from sleep. Sea-bird cries and the slap of small waves speeded his awakening. Dully he gazed up at the steep cliffs enclosing his anchorage. Sunlight burned on the highest peaks and there was no wind. Sleepily he looked at his watch, then stared with disbelief. Ten o'clock! Exhaustion, and the quiet, dark anchorage, had done him in.

He was suddenly and voraciously hungry. He stuffed himself with a roll, then ate a leathery tortilla. His hunger was like a seizure of some sort, not to be taken lightly: he had to have something solid for beakfast. But yesterday's fish, after slopping around in the bilge, was soggy and strong.

He peered down into the green depths beside the boat and saw fish hovering above a white shell floor. He pulled on trunks and began stalking his breakfast. In five minutes he had a purplish pargo on his spear. He dried off and left the cove. A haze like tobacco smoke lay on the Gulf. In a half-hour he went ashore on a little beach and broke up scraps of green-skinned *palo verde* for a fire. Then he hunched over the frying pan like a miser until the fish was cooked.

Still hungry, he stowed his dry gear and set sail. He massaged his gaunt midriff. Not only were his belly muscles sore from paddling, but he was losing weight.

The Gulf, as if anxious to prove that yesterday was merely a fit of bad temper, blew him a steady breeze, toasted him with sunshine, sent birds to dip about the mast. He sat back, smiling complacently, listening to the bow wave playing a thin, trilling music as the canoe rolled along. A school of dolphins swam beside him for a while like destroyers escorting a battleship.

At midday the hazy outline of a very large island slowly surfaced like a gray whale. Between this island and the shore he saw numerous smaller islands sprinkled about like stones. Boats were coming and going and he made out a smear of smoke over the hills.

Bahía San Jorge! Dreaming of food, and wondering suddenly about his father, he set a course for a sombrero-shaped hill at the tip of a point. Skimming the point, he saw before him a beautiful bay, blue and crab-shaped. A village lay back of the beach and palms rose in dark-green clumps. Small craft were drawn up on the sand and two shrimp boats rode at anchor in the bay. Was one of the small boats yellow? As he strained to see, a man's voice rang across the water.

"Oiga, amigo!"

Someone was standing on a massive boulder off the tip of the point, waving what looked like a butterfly net. The accent was American. Eric headed up into the wind.

"Hello!" he called.

"I'm stranded!" the man called back. "How about a lift?"

Eric had a wild hope that it was his father; but the voice and figure were wrong. "Grab the painter when I get in close," he called back.

The man, who wore felt-soled waders, came out a few feet and waited on a boulder until the boat was in reach. Catching the painter, he began to tease the boat into a wedge between two rocks. Dressed in a ragged straw hat, a short-sleeved sweatshirt, and jeans cut off at the knees, he looked like a bandy-legged little pirate. His skin was swarthy and his full cheeks dark with stubble; he wore a downcurving black moustache like a Mexican revolutionary's.

"Well, well!" he said, grinning. "An English-speaking *vagabundo!* Did you knock some fisherman on the head for his boat?"

"I traded for it at Goat Point," Eric said.

"How's Gregorio?" the man asked.

Stepping into a foot of cool water, Eric looked closely at the man. "Say, you're not the dentist he mentioned, are you?"

The man offered his hand. "At your service. Paul Nestor."

"I'm Eric Hansen—from San Diego."

"This country's full of Eric Hansens from San Diego," said the dentist, pulling a pair of chromed pliers from his pocket. "Aren't these the greatest?"

Eric grinned ruefully. "Did he know I was coming?"

"I didn't even know he had a son. What's up?"

Eric slowed down. El Rojo seemed to have developed an ability to cast spells on people. As soon as you started asking questions about him, they turned vague and defensive. He said carelessly,

"Well, I had a little time off from school, so I, uh, I came down." He squinted at the village. "Is he still here?"

"No. Too bad. He went out to the lighthouse the other day."

Sunk, but still smiling, Eric asked, "Where's that?"

Dr. Nestor's eyes, reddish-brown and vitreous, like pottery, regarded Eric steadily. Small waves lapped the boat with a slurping sound. Seconds passed. *Have I blown it already?* Eric wondered.

"The lighthouse is on Los Muertos Island," said Dr. Nestor at last. "It's been out of commission for months, and the shrimpers wanted him to try to get it going again. He's a whiz with machinery."

Eric agreed.

"He's become quite a hero with the people here," said the dentist. "They call him 'El Rojo'—the Redhead. He got the generator working at Gonzalez's store, where I'm camping, so there's electricity and refrigeration again. And he put Mrs. Gonzalez's sewing machine back in shape."

"How far is the island?" Eric asked.

"About five miles."

"Did he go out in his canoe?"

"Yep. So you thought you'd surprise him eh? Get yourself a *panga,* too, and sneak up on him?"

"Well, I had a little time . . ." *I already said that,* Eric realized. He turned to gaze out into the blue haze of the Gulf.

Dr. Nestor pointed. "The small island with a sort of chimney on the north end is Los Muertos. It's too late to go out tonight, though, if that's what you were thinking."

Eric said, gloomily, "Oh . . . Well, when do you think he'll be coming back?"

Dr. Nestor's face was raffishly amused. "As a matter of fact, he didn't say he *was* coming back. However," he added, seeing Eric's face fall, "I rather expect he will."

Eric, past faking any longer, said wearily, "Boy, I'd sure hate to miss him. It's really been a drag getting this far. Maybe I can get somebody to take me out in a power boat."

"The only power boats here are out fishing. Why don't you just loaf around till tomorrow? Then we'll work something out."

Out in the bay, Eric heard a fish splash. He chewed his lip and sighed.

Clapping a hand on his shoulder, Dr. Nestor said, "Come on, Eric—when in Baja, do as the Mexicans do. Easy does it. Now, then," as if it were all settled, "I've got a few things to take along. Or look . . ." he said. "Since you're not in a hurry, maybe we can catch a few Sally Lightfoots together. They're the main thing I came out here for, and I haven't caught one all afternoon."

Eric reached into the boat for his tennis shoes. He sat on a rock to pull them on. He had a vision of himself wandering forever down the peninsula like a tragic voyager in mythology, beset by storms, captured by crazy dentists and forced to help catch Sally Lightfoots—whatever they were—while his father sailed farther and farther from him, toward madness or a heart attack.

"What are Sally Lightfoots?" he asked.

"Crabs—the most beautiful in the world. They look like ceramics—red, blue, brown, you name it. Compared to them, lightning has iron-poor blood. I was thinking that if you took a net and got behind that big rock, I could kind of herd them toward you, and when they passed you might bag a couple."

The drenched rocks near the water line swarmed with the beautiful little crabs. Their backs resembled small shields of porcelain and their claws and legs were richly enameled. They ran nimbly on their toes; when Eric moved toward the big rock, carrying a net, crabs ten feet away took cover, moving in flocks like birds.

After he was hidden behind the rock, Dr. Nestor waited a few minutes to let the crabs forget about him. Then he began herding a covey of Sally Lightfoots toward the rock. Eric watched a few loners drift by inches out of reach.

"Okay?" called Dr. Nestor.

"Okay!"

The crabs scuttled faster. Eric poised. But the instant he started to bang the net down over a dozen of them, the whole flock made a right-angle turn toward the water and dropped over a ledge. He lunged out and charged a couple of stragglers, but they jumped aside, quick as fleas, and shot toward the water.

"Damn!" Dr. Nestor exclaimed.

They decided to work individually.

After fifteen minutes, Eric had reached the point of fretfully jabbing at them under rocks. But Dr. Nestor wanted the animals undamaged. At last Eric saw a beautiful blue crab with cloisonné legs and pincers drowsing in a pool near the water line. He crawled up on it, pounced—

"Got one!" he cried.

The crab's claws closed on his finger. He took a step backward and shook it loose. His foot slipped and he felt himself falling. Twisting, he turned the fall into a dive and hit the water.

Dr. Nestor, when he finished laughing, said that as long as he was soaked, he might as well pull on his face mask and try drifting along the water line. He told him how to hold a crab if he should catch another. Floating, Eric saw a beautiful water-world of pink sea fans, purple anemones with vicious spines like burned matchsticks, and snails with vivid mantles. He found a strange worm half hidden in a calcareous tube, on its head a ridiculous bonnet of purple plumes. At last he spotted a colony of Sallies sunning themselves near the water. He floated in, reached, grabbed.

"Got one!" he yelled. It was a lively red-backed crab, indignantly clashing its claws. Holding it from behind, thumb atop the shell, index finger beneath, he eluded the gnashing pincers. Dr. Nestor arrived with a jar and made the arrest.

Eric got five more of the little crabs by amphibious attack. Dr. Nestor praised him warmly. At three thirty, he decided it was time to go. Changing to dry clothes, Eric made a discovery that numbed him with shock.

Water had leaked into the plastic bottle containing his father's heart medicine!

"Oh, brother!" he said, displaying the little bottle of milky ooze.

"What is it?" asked the dentist.

"My father's heart medicine!"

Dr. Nestor tipped his head back and laughed. "Boy, you're too much! You didn't paddle all the way down here to deliver a bottle of pills, did you? Is that why you came?"

Scowling, Eric shook the bottle and watched the white flakes swirl like a paperweight snowstorm.

"That was part of it," he admitted.

"Why, your father's as healthy as a horse! Of course everybody in the States has some pet ailment he nurses along to forget that all he's really doing is waiting to die. I know because I was doing the same thing myself for years."

Ruffled, Eric started pulling on dry clothes. The sun lay flat upon the hills, flooding the bay with a whiskey-colored light. He saw a flash of reflected light in a cabin window of one of the shrimpers. Chuckling, Dr. Nestor carried plastic buckets and vessels to the boat. "Heart medicine!" He did not understand the situation at all; but Eric, at this point, decided he had better not mention Cresswell's fireplace if he hoped for the dentist's help.

They pushed off into the sunset breeze, which caught the boat and blew it toward the town across the bay. Dr. Nestor dipped up fresh sea water for his specimens. He had his hat off, revealing a head as bald as stone, with a ridge running down the middle of it. He looked vigorous and happy and not entirely trustworthy.

"I'll have to get word to my mother somehow," Eric said. "I haven't called her since I left San Felipe."

"No problem. In the morning I'll get the radioman on one of the shrimpers to contact a ham operator in San Diego. You can talk with her by radiotelephone. You could do it tonight, but I see they're already under way."

Eric observed that one of the sassy-looking little boats was under power, stern down and bows up, plowing a widening furrow across the bay. On the deck of the other boat, men were raising the anchor.

"It's none of my business," the dentist said, "but what's the point of all the hurry-hurry stuff? I thought you were on vacation?"

"I sort of took one because—well, there was an emergency . . ."

"Oh? I'm sorry to hear it. Anyone ill?"

His quick interest stripped the artifice from Eric. "Well, actually," he admitted, "the emergency is my father. He not only has this heart condition, but he disappeared last week!"

"How's that?"

"He just took off one night. No note—just left. He and I'd had a little beef. Nothing important, but I felt pretty lousy about it, like I'd been the one who drove him away. And Mabel—the waitress at the Coffee Shop—told me he'd eaten there the night he took off. She said his car was full of camping gear. So when I found his fishing gear gone, I figured he must have come down here. He used to tell me about a pearling expedition he and some other men made after the war. They didn't get many pearls, but they must have had a ball, because he's never stopped talking about it. It was like *Huckleberry Finn,* he said. I guess he wanted to—you know—play the scene again."

"Then why didn't you let him?" asked Dr. Nestor.

"Because we were worried about him," Eric explained patiently. "He'd never done anything like this before. And he'd been acting kind of strange, too . . ."

"I see your point," said Dr. Nestor, "but I see his, too. Just because a man's always been a house-cat type doesn't mean there isn't a little wildcat blood left in him. And if that kind of blood is kept bottled up forever, it curdles in the brain. Probably that's why he was acting 'strange.' If he'd been in the habit of taking off now and then, there'd have been no problem about his going, would there?"

"No. But he *wasn't* in the habit."

"Do you want to know what he told me?"

Eric looked at him quickly.

"He said he came down here to get degaussed. Do you know what degaussing means?"

Eric knew it had something to do with truing up a compass, that it was pronounced "degowsing." "I've heard of it."

"It means to take the magnetism out of a compass so that it will point true. What kind of trouble was it?" he asked. "Woman trouble? Finances?"

"There was no trouble. Except that maybe he didn't have enough to do. Last week he was going to buy an automobile agency, but Mom talked him out of it. But he said she was right, that he'd mess around in the grease pit while the business went to pot. So I don't know . . ."

Dr. Nestor shook his head. "But no woman trouble, eh? The woman just ran the show."

"If that's trouble," Eric shrugged. "They talked about it, and he said, 'I guess you're right.' "

"Do you want to know what's the matter?" Dr. Nestor said earnestly. "Women in the States, especially in areas like yours, have forgotten how to be women; but they haven't yet learned how to be men. They've turned into harpies, and their men into zombies. God, it's pitiful!"

Then, seeming to drop the entire subject like an overactive crab, he said, "Head for the south end of the beach, Eric, where the kids are. We'll need help carrying all this stuff into the village."

chapter **15**

As the boat floated in, a half-dozen boys ran out to help beach it. Dr. Nestor assigned loads and they hurried into the village. Against the speckled foothills, San Jorge looked drab and dusty. Tufted palms lifted above the houses; the smoke of supper fires hung like a mist in the air. Eric smelled cedar smoke and felt a pleasant coolness.

"Your things will be all right here," Dr. Nestor said. "Just bring your sleeping bag. You can spend the night with us. I'm using the porch of the store as a clinic. Gonzalez, the storekeeper, has extra cots."

They crossed the sandy beach and entered the town. Cows

wandered about, roosters crowed, a rusty windmill creaked. An old bull and a young one stood rubbing heads together with a hollow clacking of horns. The haphazard arrangement of fishermen's *jacales* gave a mere suggestion of streets.

They came to a square lined with adobe huts on four sides to form a tiny plaza. In the middle was a stone well surrounded by benches and some lacy desert trees. A burro heaped with kindling crossed the plaza with mincing steps as an old man switched its heels. Barelegged girls hurried along with buckets of water balanced on their heads. Dr. Nestor led the way to a long adobe building where a dusty red camper with enormous doughnut tires was backed up to one of its long porches.

While Dr. Nestor found coins for the boys, Eric gazed around. Two porches came together in an L, wide and airy and furnished with chairs and tables and a few homemade beds like monstrous army cots. Vines partially screened the porches. There were a dozen cage birds and some big-leaved plants growing in rusty five-gallon cans. A pink cardinal near him ruffled its feathers. He smelled fish frying. He had had only tortillas to eat since breakfast, and hunger suddenly roared out at him like a lion.

Dr. Nestor started arranging his containers on a table. "I'll be preserving specimens till after dark," he said, "so you'd better eat. Polly!" he called.

A girl in a white nylon uniform appeared in the door. "Hi! Do any good?" she asked. Seeing Eric, she smiled. "Oh, you're back—" Then she stared. "Excuse me! I thought you were—"

"This is Mr. Hansen's son, Eric," said her father. "My daughter, Polly, Eric."

Eric went toward her, tingling with surprise and pleasure. She was exceptionally tall, nearly six feet, and strikingly pretty. *Beautiful,* he decided. Her blonde hair fell nearly to her waist in a single heavy braid. She wore an orange band over her head. Nicely toasted by the sun, her skin was so smooth that it looked poreless. Her eyes, very large, were green and had the faintly bewildered expression of near-sighted girls who refuse to wear glasses.

He thought of a white queen, an Amazon, a statue of a frontier girl. How had Dr. Nestor failed to mention having such a daughter? Clearly it was the most important thing about him.

She offered Eric her hand. It was warm and wet, as her father's had been clammy. She wiped it on her uniform. "I've been sterilizing instruments. Are you really Mr. Hansen's son? Well, you *have* to be—you look just like him. I mean—except younger."

He was pleased to notice that she was as excited as he was. He was also confirmed in his guess of near-sightedness, if she could mistake him for his father.

"Dinner's almost ready," said Polly. "I cleaned a fisherman's teeth and he gave us a sierra."

"Feed Eric generously," her father told her, "but save some for me. He's going to stay with us tonight. How about a hand with this table, Eric?"

After they had moved the table close to the camper, Dr. Nestor arranged bottles and trays on it. Polly brought him a cup of coffee and he sat down to work. Eric found a basin, a jug and a mirror. He washed up and came back, his hair neatly combed for the first time in days.

"It's ready," Polly called from the camper.

Lights burned brightly within the camper. It was large and comfortable, with seats that made into beds, cooking equipment, and a chrome chest of dental instruments. Two places had been set at the table. He was surprised to observe that Polly had changed to a skirt and blouse. They sat down, acutely aware of each other. Eric was giddy with the sight and smell of food—buttery fish, a fresh vegetable, hot tortillas. He tried to pace himself, to eat like a gentleman as some men made an effort to drink like gentlemen, but soon he was eating with both hands and making garbled replies to Polly's conversational efforts. At last, winded, he sat back and patted his stomach with both hands.

"Good chow, Polly."

Polly said coyly, "Oh, anybody can fry fish."

Eric heard Dr. Nestor talking to himself as he worked.

"What's your father do with all the goop we brought back?" he asked.

"He has a crazy project on. He thinks there's something special about animals that prefer rough water when there's calm water right around the corner. Yesterday there was a storm surf, so he had to get right out there today and catch a lot of specimens in their *absolute prime*. Leaving me to clean teeth. He's going to make a vaccine from their blood and inoculate people so *they're* tougher, too."

"You're kidding!" Eric glanced out the door.

Polly giggled. "Well, something like that. Pure scientific curiosity, I guess. 'Is tenacity innate or acquired?' is how he puts it."

Eric gloated—the soft seat, the good food, the beautiful girl. "How come you live down here?" he asked. "Don't you go to school?"

"I'm a senior in Baja High. Correspondence course, actually. When I graduate, the school has to send me a diploma, a date, and a corsage."

"What if they don't?" asked Eric.

"I'll drink Dad's formaldehyde," she said grimly. "Truly, though, I like Baja. The Malaria Parade—beautiful! All those yellow faces. And the Cactus Festival . . . ! They stick candles on the branches of the elephant tree and dance for three days and nights while I try to sleep."

Eric laughed. "Do you live here all the time?"

"I come down now and then. Then I go back to San Francisco and stay with my mother."

Mystery here, Eric thought.

"How can your father make a living taking care of poor people's teeth?" he asked.

Polly sipped from a bottle of Coke. "There isn't much money in it, but there's a lot of chicken and dried shark meat. We keep it in the safe."

Eric was aware that he was not getting many straight answers.

"How far south does he travel?" he asked.

"To Todos Santos, near the tip on the Pacific side. And north to Goat Point." She propped her chin on her fists. "Why are *you* down here, Eric? Are you a dropout?"

Eric took another pastry and regarded it thoughtfully. Those beautiful green eyes gazed at him, making him tingle.

"I needed a little break. Came down to Goat Point on my motorcycle, then switched over to a canoe. Kicks," he said, offhandedly.

"Won't you flunk?"

"If I do, I'll make it up in summer school. I'll be going back in a couple of days."

Polly looked disappointed. But in a moment she brought up another smile. "What's your college major going to be?" she asked.

"Coincidence," Eric said. "Marine biology!"

"Really? You should stay here awhile. Dad says the Gulf is like a giant marine laboratory. There are varieties that don't exist anywhere else in the world."

Eric thought of one Baja variety—his father. "Interesting," he said.

"I still think you're a dropout, though," Polly said, peering at him. "I'll bet you're wanted for selling pot on the schoolgrounds."

Eric grinned. "Lay a lid on you for a peso, kid," he said.

"And your father—so *nice*—but it's funny he didn't mention that he had a family. Bet he's a dropout, too."

"Very flattering that he forgot us," said Eric. "That's why I came down—to remind him that he has a family. No, actually," he said quickly, "I just decided that if he could take a vacation, so could I."

Polly smiled, but her eyes had narrowed thoughtfully. She nibbled a pastry, gazing intently at the back of his skull through his eyes. Evidently deciding that she had pursued her investigation far enough, she said,

"Aren't you afraid at night? Just you against Baja?"

"I sleep like a baby."

"You mean you wake up every four hours and eat? I believe it! What an appetite. I've got a boy friend in San Francisco named Eric. Isn't that odd? What's your girl friend's name?"

Wow, he thought, *she's really turned on! Doesn't get much chance to talk,* he deduced. "Joanie," he said. He heard an engine start; lights flickered on inside Gonzalez's store: The generator, restored to life by El Rojo. Glancing out the window, he was surprised to see that it was dark.

"We had a big hassle before I left," he said thoughtfully.

She glanced at him. "Who? You and Joanie?"

"Yeah. Dumb broad."

"What about?"

"That's the funny part—I can't really explain it. I called her up two nights before I left. I wanted—support, I guess you'd call it. All I got was some stupid advice. She sounded like her mother. I can't explain it. But I hung up on her."

"That's the worst kind of argument!" Polly said. "When you don't know what you're fighting about. It's terrible, isn't it?" But she sounded cheerful, and patted her hair in back.

"Awful," Eric said, with a grin. He went outside to see about his bed. Dr. Nestor had left his worktable, but Eric saw him standing with a little crowd of people in the street. The dentist beckoned to him.

"What do you think?" he said. "The lighthouse is working!"

Everyone was pointing at a tiny gold bead lying on the dark velvet of the Gulf and blinking on and off. El Rojo had come through! Learning that the son of El Rojo was present, everyone came up and shook Eric's hand and told him how clever his father was. It came to him that there was a puzzle here: the very talent that made his father a hero in Baja was worth practically nothing at home. About all it had done for him was to bring a warning by the local police force not to exercise it.

chapter **16**

In the morning the birds woke Eric.

Near his cot, over and over, the pink cardinal warbled a woody song that made him smile in his sleep. Other birds chirped and trilled as though the greatest day in history were breaking, and they had been invited to greet it. He thought of a line from Chaucer, something about "little birds, a goodly number." There were a goodly number on Gonzalez's porch, and they succeeded in bringing him wide awake.

Then the problems of the day gathered about his bed like vultures. He stared at the brushwood ceiling, frowning in anguish.

Call Mother. Head for Los Muertos. Hope for good weather. Decide what to do if El Rojo, that exasperating migratory redbird, had flown south again. In his brain, the fretful nerve fussed like a child with a runny nose.

Sounds in the camper. Polly tiptoed out in a robe, heading for the bathroom in the store. Returned and washed up. He watched. She did her braid up on top of her head, leaned close to the mirror and squinted. Exclaimed under her breath, let it fall again in a golden hawser. Some tall girls were sensitive about their height. It added ugly inches, he supposed. She tiptoed back to the camper.

Soon he smelled coffee. Breakfast was preparing itself, as the Mexicans said. Wonderful. He did not have to stir a hand. Much to be said for the squaw system.

Next Dr. Nestor emerged, laying a hand on Eric's shoulder as he passed. "Hit the deck, skipper!"

They ate scrambled eggs with Mexican sausage at the table where Dr. Nestor had worked last night. A small flock of goats passed in the street, herded by a brown and white dog.

"See that dog?" said Dr. Nestor. "That's a *chiverro*—half dog, half goat. *Chiva,* goat; *perro,* dog; *chiverro.*"

Eric looked. "It just looks like a dog," he said.

"He's raised with goats from the day he's born. A nanny nurses him. By the time he's grown, he thinks he *is* a goat. He takes the flock out every morning, brings it back at night. He drives off the flock's enemies. He gets fed here, or he probably wouldn't bother to come back. Only one guy loses on the deal."

Eric watched the dog fret the last of the goats along the road.

"The dog who thinks he's a goat," said Dr. Nestor. "He can't even chase a rabbit without leaving a note to say where he's gone . . . Well, what's your schedule today?" he asked briskly.

Eric got the point, still did not buy it. A man was not a dog.

"I've been thinking," he said, "that I'll have to go out to the lighthouse before I call my mother. I'd have to call after I get back anyway because I don't know anything now."

"Right."

"I'd better try to find a motorboat. Since Dad's got the light working, he probably won't be hanging around long. I want to get out there as fast as I can."

"Maybe you'd like Polly to go along," Dr. Nestor suggested. "She can show you where to beach your boat. The light's a mile or so from the beach."

Eric looked at her. She smiled and waited. "Can you cut classes?" he asked.

"If you want me to go. I can make it up later," Polly said. She started clearing the table.

Patients had begun showing up, silently taking their places against the leafy lattice wall. They were humble country people in work clothes. The men wore their collars buttoned; many of the women brought one end of their black *rebozos* over their mouths. One of the men, short, rough-looking, unshaven, squatted down and lit a cigarette. An old blue yachting cap sat back on his rumpled black hair. He winked at Eric and blew smoke in the air. The men smoked differently, here, Eric noticed; they held the cigarette warily, as though it were a caterpillar, puffing slowly and infrequently, not gasping and blowing as though they had only fifteen seconds on the butt before passing it to the next man.

Dr. Nestor spoke to this man. "Not fishing today, Luis?"

"Maybe later."

"This *joven* needs a boat. Will you take him out to Los Muertos?"

The fisherman looked Eric over. "Sure. Ten dollars."

"It's a deal," Eric said.

Dr. Nestor took Luis first. He rigged a lightweight dental chair, a little table of instruments, and a drill powered by a battery-operated electric motor. Working slowly and calmly, he talked with the fisherman and the others waiting, sipping coffee now and then. Children played about the porch. Dr. Nestor installed two silver fillings for the man and collected a few pesos.

Carrying a picnic basket, Polly came from the camper in white capris and a red blouse. Her hair shone like silk. Eric longed to get his hands on her braid—squeeze it, pull it. Echoes of childhood; Little League sadism.

Dr. Nestor brought the Sally Lightfoots from the refrigerator. "Will you do something for me? Take these Sallies back and turn them loose. I've tagged them. Six months from now I'll look for them again on that ledge and see if they're still alive and hearty."

With a jug of water, the picnic hamper, and some supplies for the lighthousekeeper, they set out in Luis's boat. White with red trim, it planed smoothly with a big outboard motor bawling behind it. The tranquil green plane of the Gulf rolled out like a desert of jade. There was a hot, hazy sky with slots of blue. Each time Eric glanced back at Luis, the fisherman would grin at him, a wet cigarette in the corner of his mouth, and wink.

Eric returned the Sally Lightfoots to the rock. Then they headed on. Later they saw some flying fish, then a couple of giant manta rays leaping from the water and falling back with a huge splash. Luis decided to chase one. He picked up the iron harpoon at his feet and offered it to Eric, who declined. The Mexican laughed. While Eric chewed his lip in frustration, time bleeding away, the fisherman wasted twenty minutes dodging around among the devilfish.

At last they reached Los Muertos, a small crag of volcanic rock battered by the sea. On its south side lay a small beach. A few goats grazed on salt grass. A chimney of rock rose at the north end of the island, a whitewashed tower atop it. The only landing, Luis yelled, was at the beach. Everything had to be carried up from there. A government ship brought supplies now and then—butane for the light, food for Elijo, the keeper of the light.

Eric stood up as they headed for the beach, scanning the volcanic cove in which the beach nestled like a moonstone. A rowboat lay on the sand; there were remains of another boat high and dry. But no yellow *panga*. Polly chewed on her braid.

"He *might* have hidden it in the brush . . ." she said.

Eric shook his head. With sudden anger, he turned to Luis, pointing down the Gulf.

"How much to take me down there? Half a day down, half a day back?"

Unscrewing the cap from his gas tank, Luis peered in, thrust in a finger, and shook his head. *"No se puede."*

Red-faced, Eric spread his arms, furious at fate, at the Mexican, at El Rojo. "It's nearly full! Don't give me that." He was surprised to hear himself making all this noise.

Luis raised his shoulders and turned up empty hands. No can do. The boat cruised slowly toward the sand.

Eric sputtered in outrage. "But you knew—you should have filled up . . ."

Luis's dark eyes glazed with displeasure. Just then the boat grounded; Eric, facing the stern, lost his balance. He saw the Mexican's face break into a grin as he did a backflip onto a heap of jackets and canvas. Even so, the wind was knocked out of him. Polly hurried to help. Angrily he gestured her away.

In silence they beached the boat and unloaded. Polly waved at someone near the lighthouse a half-mile distant.

"There's Elijo," she said. "You still want to talk to him, don't you? And find out where your father went . . . ?"

Eric said, "Yeah. I'll have to let Elijo play his big scene."

"What's that?"

"Where he shows me the pliers my old man gave him."

They climbed from the beach to the cliff, then hiked north to the lighthouse. The tower was glazed on all sides, each window polished. Chickens wandered about; a dog barked at them. Wearing clean suntans, the keeper of the light came to meet them, a fine old man, dignified but friendly. He accepted with thanks the things they had brought him. When Polly introduced Eric as the son of El Rojo, Elijo clasped Eric's hand.

"My house is yours! Come inside—I must show you something."

They played the pliers scene.

Eric had not the heart to seem anything but surprised and pleased. He pretended to pull a tooth with the HanDeeRench, then handed it back.

"When did my father leave?" he asked.

"Well, let's see. Last night was the first night the light operated. But he didn't come yesterday, he came the day before. No, the day before *that*. He swam and fished for a day. Then he fixed the light and left."

"That was day before yesterday?"

"Exactly."

"Where was he going?"

"To Bahía Escondida."

"How far is that?"

Elijo and Luis conferred. Elijo gazed out the window at the blue vacancy of water stretching to the south. All the water in the world, thought Eric, and sixteen feet of slow boat. . . .

"Well, in a *panga*—five days. Three hundred kilometers, maybe. There's nothing between here and there but a few *vagabundo* camps."

Two hundred miles, Eric thought in shock.

End of the voyage.

Finished.

Final.

"A fine man, your father," said Elijo. And, turning over favorite memories of that living legend, he frowned and put two fingers over his mouth. "He was sick the last night. I made him a turtle *machaca, muy brava.* Maybe he ate too much. I heard him pacing around and groaning. But he was all right in the morning. A little pale, maybe. . . ."

Eric thought, And now I suppose he's down the coast a few miles, looking pale, and drifting.

Elijo showed them his light, the burnished reflectors, the butane tanks. He exhibited a framed congratulatory letter from the Governor for his years of service. He told stories of wrecks on the reefs between Los Muertos and the big island a few miles east, El Indio. Elijo and Luis exchanged legends of ships sunk between here and Bahía Escondida, the Hidden Bay. Pirates had lurked in Bahía Escondida in those days, preying on government ships collecting treasure from the missions up and down the peninsula.

But Eric's heart was not in the fun. Presently he suggested that he and Polly go down and have a swim. Luis said he would eat with Elijo. No hurry, was there? Too late to leave today, since Eric had to return, radio his mother, and buy food if he were going.

No hurry, Eric agreed. It was only his father's life they were dribbling away.

Polly went behind a shrub and put on her bathing suit, a blue one-piece that she filled as snugly as a Boy Scout's knapsack. Watching her stand in a foot of water while he pulled on his trunks behind the bush, the only one on the beach, Eric's state of mind improved. When he was dressed, he sneaked across the sand, then rushed into the water, yelling and splashing her. Polly screamed and hugged herself. Good kid! he thought. Joanie was inclined to ignore him, then drop him with a ball of wet sand when he turned his back.

In the warm water his woes melted like sugar.

They floated on their backs, watching scissor-tailed frigate birds ride the breeze. They dived to the bottom and chased colorful tropicals among the rocks studding the clean sand. So clear was the water that even without a face mask everything looked bright. The bluish light made Polly's lips appear orange. She held up a snowy cockleshell. He took it, then on impulse dropped it and seized her by the hair. She batted her eyes questioningly and tried to pull away, but he drew her close and kissed her orange lips.

They swam up and she switched her wet braid at him. "Don't think just because—because . . ."

Eric submerged and seized her by the ankles. Faintly he heard her scream. He pulled her under, bubbles trailing from her mouth. When he let her go, she swam furiously after him. Eric fled, frog-style, but turned suddenly to meet her head on.

What am I doing? he thought. Do I want to start this?

The point was, it was only for today. Then he'd be gone.

Polly eluded him, surfaced, and started paddling away, but Eric overtook her. She screamed when he caught her ankles again. He let her get another breath before he swarmed over her and carried her under. He wriggled until he got his arms around her. She kept turning her head, but did not push him away. This time he kissed her soundly; her hands came up and touched his shoulders, then moved away. He grasped her by the waist, ran his palms up her ribs.

She pulled away vigorously. They floated up and treaded water, looking at each other.

"Are you sore?" Eric asked, pawing water from his eyes.

"Certainly." She swished her braid at his face. "Animal!"

"I couldn't help it."

"I could tell you were trying." She looked at him in a grave, hurt way that said, *You know I'm lonesome, and there aren't any other boys, so you think you can get away with anything.*

"Put yourself in my place," he said. "Fighting my way down the coast—and suddenly there she is! The White Queen!"

"Any girl would have looked like a queen to you. Sailors can't be choosey." She looked genuinely indignant. The more she thought about it, the angrier she seemed to get.

Eric showed all his teeth suddenly in a shark-grin, and reached for her shoulders, but she ducked, surfaced ten feet away, and swam toward shore. This time she really swam. Before he overtook her she was in the shallows. She got up and ran for the beach. Eric chased her. Suddenly she stopped and waited for him, hands on hips, her face haughty.

"You saw Elijo's big spyglass, didn't you, Animal?" she said. "They're watching every move we make. I might even scream."

Eric raised his eyes to the lighthouse. "You're probably right," he said. Dropping his hands, he gazed up and down the beach. "It's still a great beach. No lifeguards, no people."

"Let's eat," Polly said. "Maybe it will settle you down."

On a beach towel yards square, they ate the lunch she had

brought. He studied her. Her eyes were a deep Christmas-tree green. Her golden skin gleamed with salt crystals. Naturally, being a dentist's daughter, her teeth were matched like a row of Chiclets. Aside from being very pretty, and the only American girl within hundreds of miles, there was an undefinable quality about her that made him tingle all over. He liked the way she talked, the way she looked at him when she was not being haughty.

Watch out! he told himself. It's no time to be falling in love.

"Have you ever been a queen?" he asked her. "Like a roller derby queen? Or junior class queen?"

"I was elected queen of the Cactus Festival at San Felipe last year. But when I saw the crown, I withdrew my name."

"No, really."

"Really, no. But thanks for nominating me. Big blondes don't get elected, only little dark-haired girls. Plus, I don't stay anywhere long enough to get elected to anything. I'm an orphan of the trail. I'll go back after Dad finishes this run. Summers are pretty horrible down here."

"Why does he stay?"

She evaded his gaze. "It's a 'calling,' I guess. He likes the people and wants to help them. He doesn't even pay expenses; most of his money comes from what he'd saved before he came down. And then his project—he's really serious about those rough-water animals."

Eric lay on his back with a handful of corn chips. "If this goes on any longer," he said, "I'll be a new breed of rough-water animal."

Polly lay on her stomach, looking at him. "What will you do now?"

"Brother. Wish I knew. I'll talk to my mother and let her decide."

"You're so close . . ." said Polly, trickling sand through

her fingers. "It's fabulous country between here and Bahía Escondida. If you go, you won't be bored. Dad took me down in a boat last year. There are beautiful little coves, and fishing you wouldn't believe. And we dived for pearls at one place. It's the most gorgeous diving spot I've ever seen. Green water, white shell beach. . . . I kind of envy you."

The food and the sun were exacting energy from him. He was almost too drowsy to worry. He turned over and lay face down beside her. His elbow brushed blue cloth and golden skin. Her expression, he saw suddenly, was sad; her eyes brooded. He tapped her arm and she looked at him.

"What's on your mind, blonde?" he said.

"I was thinking about *my* father."

"He seems happy enough."

"He makes himself happy. But he'd like to go back."

"Why doesn't he, then?"

"He can't," Polly said.

"Why not?"

"The Feds."

Eric raised his head. "What?"

"He's wanted."

"You're kidding!"

"Don't breathe a word! I get so lonesome I have to talk to somebody, or I wouldn't be telling you. I'm not sure of the details. He was in a business deal with some other men, just financing it, actually, but he was involved. Something about using the mails. . . . He's been here six years; another six to go. Statute of limitations."

Eric lowered his head onto his arms. He thought about it. Girls were great at fantasying, but she sounded pretty serious. "Rough," he said. "He doesn't seem like a crook."

Polly punched his arm. "He isn't a crook! I told you."

"I mean, uh—he seems pretty relaxed and all, for a guy on the lam."

They were silent.

"The problem of parental delinquency," Eric said. "Where did we fail them?"

Polly smiled drowsily.

"I wonder if my old man knows I'm chasing him," Eric yawned.

"Probably. The radiomen on the shrimp boats talk together all the time. We pick up their calls in the camper. So they've probably told him you're on his trail."

"Then I'll *never* catch up with him."

"Why is it so important?"

Eric hesitated over how to make the matter clear. "He's got this heart condition, you see. If he got sick down here, he'd probably die before they could get him to a doctor. And he had a kind of nervous condition—" He told her about the last week in Rancho Sereno.

"My goodness!" Polly said. "That *was* kind of odd."

"What do they call it when a person has these highs and lows? Anyway, I figure he's on a high now. Paddling around having a ball, making a hero of himself. That's great, but what happens when the swing starts down? He might—well, he might kill himself."

"No!" Polly said. "Not him. He seemed so happy—not high, just happy. I can't imagine his doing anything like that."

"You haven't seen him when he was low. And I want to talk to him about the whole deal—why he split, and other things. If I'd kept out of it, it probably wouldn't have happened."

Polly said, with a smile, "Oh, you're just a worry wart."

"I hope so."

chapter **17**

It was late afternoon when Luis sauntered down the path, cry-
ing, *"Vámonos!"* They shoved off, rounded the foot of the
island, and headed into the sun. The light splintered into gems
on the dark-blue water. Eric went back to shout at Luis.

"Will you stop at one of the shrimpers on the way in?"

Luis nodded. A half-hour later, as they entered the bay, he
made for the first of the boats, a white boat with the pilothouse
well forward, her sides stained with rust. Laundry hung from
the rigging. Dark-skinned fishermen leaned on the bulwarks
watching them come alongside. One of them caught the
painter Eric tossed and held the skiff while he clambered
aboard. A big unshaven man in a straw hat and dungarees, his

tee shirt molded over an ample belly, came from the pilot-house chewing on a piece of black cigar. He spoke rapidly in English.

"Yes, hello! I'm Captain Gallardo. *Mucho gusto*. Dr. Nestor told me about you. I've managed to contact a radio operator in San Diego. *Apúrese!*"

Eric hurried up the scaly deck after him toward the wheel-house. A small table was bolted to a bulkhead of the cabin. On it rested a radio, scratched and rusty, a hand microphone, and a pair of headphones. The captain told Eric to sit down and put on the headphones.

"Press this switch to talk, this one to listen."

Eric heard sounds like an orchestra of musical saws tuning up. A man's voice came through indistinctly, repeating certain phrases.

". . . Ship *Estrella del Mar*. Are you still there? *Estrella del Mar*—"

Eric pushed the microphone switch. "This is Eric Hansen, on the *Estrella del Mar!*"

Polly entered and took the chair Captain Gallardo offered her. The man in San Diego came in again, told him to stand by, and Eric heard a telephone being dialed. Suddenly, across the deserts and mountains, he heard his mother's voice, wavery but clear and commanding.

"This is Ruth Hansen. Hello?"

"Hello, Mom," Eric said.

"Eric! Where in heaven—"

"I'm in a place called Bahía San Jorge. It's about, well, two hundred and fifty miles below the border."

"*Why* haven't you *called*?"

"There was no place to call, Mom."

"Is there a landing strip?"

Eric repeated the question to the captain, who nodded.

"Yes," Eric told his mother.

"Pancho Vincent will fly down for you tomorrow. Just stay put. Don't move an inch."

"Don't you want to know what I've been doing?" Eric asked, nettled. What did she think, he was on a cruise?

"Of course. But I also want to know what you're *going* to be doing. What about your father?"

Eric felt his temper rising. He fingered the blisters on his palm and thought of the terrible day when it blew.

"I don't know about Dad," he said sullenly. "I haven't caught up with him yet."

Her exasperated sigh was clearly audible.

"You don't know?" she said. "Nearly a week, and you don't know?"

"This isn't downtown San Diego, Mom," Eric retorted. "This is Nowhereville, Mexico. I keep just missing him."

"Don't you *hear* anything about him?"

"Yeah, they love him. He's passing out HanDeeRenches and repairing their broken-down motors and stuff."

"Well, I'm glad he's having fun. But I'm not going to lose both my men down there. Pancho was going to fly down tomorrow anyway and start looking for you if I hadn't heard. He'll leave early and probably be in about eleven. Tell me the name of the place again. Spell it."

Polly was looking at him intently. As their eyes met, she gave a little smile and twiddled her thumbs in her lap.

"Bahía San Jorge." He spelled it. "It's a fishing town. *What?* There *aren't* any hotels here, Mom! I don't *need* a room! What do you think I've been doing up to now, having maid service? Oh, by the way, I traded the Ossa for a dugout canoe."

A hush.

"It was the only way to follow him, Mom," he argued. "The roads down here aren't that great, you know."

"Then how did your father keep going?"

"He traded the Riley for a boat. His is yellow, mine is blue."

He thought he heard Polly snicker. Encouraged, he picked up the microphone and tilted back in the chair. Captain Gallardo, chewing on his cigar, gazed out the window, smiling.

"He was drunk," Mrs. Hansen stated categorically.

"He can't still be drunk, and he's still paddling. Incidentally, his heart medicine got wet, and—"

"Well, that's one worry we don't have, at least. Dr. Edwards told me his heart tests were fine. Do you remember how red his face was? He'd given him cortisone for tennis elbow and it tends to make one flush. So that's all that was." Clearing the decks with a little cough, she said briskly, "Well, now, are we clear on everything . . . ?"

"Listen, Mom. I think I'd better give it another couple of days. He's gone on down to—" His plans developing as he talked, Eric decided to go slow on giving out facts. "They didn't know the name, but it's down the coast a few days. It's the kind of place he'd be likely to stay, the lighthousekeeper said."

"Who said?"

"He got the lighthouse working on an island here. The old man out there told me he thought he'd probably stay at this other place for a few days."

"I hope he has a lovely time. But *you're* coming back tomorrow. This is ridiculous! You've already lost a full week of school—"

"I can make it up."

"If you're saying that you intend to keep following him, it's out of the question."

"A few days more won't matter," Eric insisted. "And if he's

slipped a cog or something, I'd better find it out and try to talk him into coming back, hadn't I? I'll head south full bore tomorrow morning. I can call you from there, the same way I did here. I'm on a shrimp boat."

A hesitation. Then: "Why don't you charter the boat?"

"I haven't got enough money, for one thing. And if I wait for Pancho, I'll be another full day behind."

"Pancho can fly you down to—what's the name of the town?"

"I didn't get it. Look, if I come on big that way, Dad may get stubborn. You know how he is. But if I come paddling up and he knows I've done it the hard way, I think he'll listen to me."

"Well. . . . Oh, heavens. What a mess!"

Eric heard an engine start, felt a grinding throb under the deck. "I'd better get off the line or I'll be going seining tonight," he said. "I'll call you. Okay?"

"Oh, all right. Wait—! Are you purifying the water before you drink it?"

"When I can get water."

Afterward, Eric tried to pay the captain, but the man declined the money. They shook hands. Captain Gallardo escorted them to the side of the boat and they took off for the beach. Eric leaned close to Polly and shouted:

"Not that paddling a dugout is that much fun! But she didn't seem to realize I worked like a dog getting this far. And then to have somebody come down and fly me back in a couple of hours . . ." He shook his head in disgust.

"Do you know what you're getting into?" Dr. Nestor said. "Two hundred miles by sail and paddle is quite an undertaking."

"I got this far," Eric said. He tore off a bite of hard roll and set to work chewing. The small victory over his mother had left him feeling upbeat.

"If you really want the truth, I envy you," Dr. Nestor confided. "There're some great diving spots between here and Bahía Escondida. Remember the place where we dived for pearl oysters?" he asked Polly.

"*Do* I!" She sighed. "Even if oysters were all we got."

Though she smiled at Eric, a shadow of regret hung between them. He, too, suddenly felt let down, the excitement leaking out of him with an almost audible hiss. He had been determined not to let his enjoyment of her grow into anything more complicated. And here he was at the very edge of the old, familiar souvenir-saving madness. . . . Six months ago he had finally discarded the last relics of a madness called Diane—some scraps of theatre tickets, a dried flower, a ribbon she had once worn in her hair.

Her mouth downturned, Polly said to her father, "Did Mr. Zaragoza come in town?"

"He sent word that he'll be here day after tomorrow."

"Can you wait?"

"I don't have much choice, since he also sent word that he has a toothache. This is an old farmer patient of mine," Dr. Nestor told Eric. "Well, it doesn't matter much. I'm stuck here with some elaborate restoration work for the next couple of days anyway. And after I leave, it'll be that long dull drive to Bahía Escondida, with only one stop in between. Any girl in her right mind would say, 'Lots of luck, Pops,' and go with Eric."

Eric's head came up. He saw a spark of playfulness in the dentist's olive-black eyes. Was he serious?

"Okay, Pops!" Polly said brightly. "Lots of luck."

Eric tingled all over. Of course they were only joking—-but were they?

"Actually," Dr. Nestor said, "the idea isn't so bizarre. You did take judo instead of folk dancing at school for two years, so you'd be perfectly safe."

Polly's face colored. "Dad, have you snapped your cap?" she asked.

Dr. Nestor winked at Eric. "She's good company," he said, "and strong as a horse. She could cook, paddle, and mend your moccasins. Couldn't you use a deckhand?"

"What are you doing, trying to marry me off?" Polly demanded.

"Who's talking about marriage? If you behaved yourselves, the subject would never come up. The fact is, it's a wretched trip by car. Plus, you'd be along to point out to Eric the best camping spots, and keep him from getting small-boat fever. Also, I think you need a change."

The prospect of Polly's coming along started Eric's heart knocking against his ribs. He plunged before he could freeze up.

"How about it?" he said to her. "There's plenty of room . . ."

She dropped both hands in her lap and looked at her father. "Well, *I* don't know!" she exclaimed. "I'm not afraid of being taken advantage of, to use Mother's term. What do you *really* think, Dad?"

Dr. Nestor laughed. "I've been telling you what I think. I really think you should do it."

"Well, I guess it's settled!" Polly said, seeming exasperated. She still had not looked directly at Eric. "You'd better get us some things from the store. Heavy on the canned fruit juice. Oh, and some of those homemade sugar lumps. They ought to be good for quick energy."

Eric felt that he, personally, had all the energy at this moment that he could handle.

Polly's father said, "Let's see what we can find, Eric," and got up from the table. Eric followed him into the store.

The interior was murkily lit by a naked light globe that pulsed with surges of power from the generator. While Gonzalez, the fat storekeeper, weighed crackers from an open sack, Dr. Nestor said:

"Actually, I'm more worried about your welfare than hers. Remember—she's a female, and full of tricks. She'll have you dropping anchor so she can do a water color of an island, or heaven knows what. I've probably spoiled her a little. So defend yourself at all times."

Eric grinned. Men liked to talk about women as though they had some sort of special malignant power, a witchlike ability to control men. But Polly was honest and open, a real sweet kid. Joanie had some of the witch in her, and would do mean things just to make you burn. Leave you waiting on the telephone and pretend she'd forgotten you were on the line; keep you waiting fifteen minutes when you called to pick her up. But she and Polly were entirely different creatures.

"She doesn't worry me," he said. "It'll be great to have her along."

chapter 18

In the rosy dawn they loaded the boat. The *chiverro* dog passed with his flock of bleating goats, looking busy and anxious, burdened by responsibility. A club of buzzards with naked red heads huddled nearby, waiting for scraps of refuse.

Without being asked, Polly washed down the bilge with a bucket of sea water and a couple of dirty sponges that had come with the boat. Eric stepped the mast and she caught one of the lines swinging loose.

"Do you want this made fast? I think it's the forestay."

"You're pretty smart," Eric said. "Make it so."

They rigged the sails, stowed provisions, and loaded jugs of water. Polly had brought a plump red nylon bag of clothing. Some boys stood by to push them off. Polly threw her arms around her father's neck.

" 'Bye, old one!" she said. "Lock yourself in at night."

"Good-bye, baby." Dr. Nestor shook Eric's hand. "I'm counting on you, Skipper."

"Bet your last buck on this baby," Eric said.

Polly stepped into the boat. Eric told her to sit in the bow. Handing her one of the paddles, he took his place in the stern. "You won't have to paddle long," he promised. "Just long enough to get us under way, not build up any muscles."

The boys shoved them off. Gamely, the little boat breasted the tiny waves. *Two hundred miles!* Eric thought. *Judas Priest.* On the other hand, ten hours a day at four knots was over forty miles a day. Say five days at the most. They waved and set to paddling. Polly paddled well. She said she had learned to canoe at summer camps. Her motions were neat and graceful, what Debbie's horse trainer called "collected." He enjoyed watching her. For some time there was only the gurgle of bubbles under the hull.

"What's the boat's name?" asked Polly.

"I don't think she has one."

"Every boat has a name! My goodness. We'll have to name her quickly, or there'll be bad luck."

"Fine," Eric said. "U.S.S. *Quickly.*"

Polly giggled. "That sounds like a minesweeper."

She suggested various names. *Sea Gull. Sea Breeze. Sea Bird.* Suddenly there was a rippling of water near the boat and a blowing sound at the left. They looked around. Polly pointed in delight.

"Dolphins!"

A dozen of the graceful animals were swimming along

within yards of the boat. Through the blue water Eric could see the shapes of others. One, very small, nuzzled the side of the canoe and a larger one quickly shooed it off. They stayed with the boat for an hour. Eric could not get over the novelty of them, their grace and exuberance. By the time they left, the choice of a name was unanimous: *Delfina,* Spanish for dolphin.

Through the morning the wind rose, then held warm and steady. At noon Polly unwrapped some sandwiches she had brought. After lunch, yawning, Polly said, "Sack time, Captain. Okay?"

She lay on the floor and fell asleep. Eric gazed at her, fondly. When she awoke, she decided to take a swim. She towed behind the boat for a while, then traded places with Eric. The water was cool and tangy, but he was disturbed by the blue darkness below him, uneasily aware of its depth, as he was conscious of height when he looked down from the top of a high building. In either case, you were dead when you hit bottom.

It was three o'clock when he climbed back in the boat. With hours of sailing still ahead, he was tired. He showed Polly an island far down the coast that he was navigating by and gave her the tiller. Sleep was elusive, but when it came he slept hard, wearing himself out. His anxieties knotted up in him like wet string. He knew in his heart that he would never catch up with his father; that if he did catch him he would be unable to persuade him to return. He had bitten off more than he could chew. He struggled in a dream cavern; strange, threatening fears swam big and slow and dark about him. Panicky, he floated up to half-consciousness. The dark fish-shapes somehow symbolized his helplessness and ineptitude.

He tore himself from sleep with a whimper. His eyes opened. The light was amber, now—late afternoon. His heart pounded. Still haunted by the sharklike fears of that deeper sea of his mind, he rose to his knees and splashed water in his face from the bow. He knew he must have been making sounds in his sleep. But when he looked at Polly, she was peering down the coast in a businesslike fashion.

"You really slept. Feel better?"

He felt stupid and slow. "I guess so." He glanced at his watch. He had slept for over an hour.

"There's a cove below us. It looks like a good place to stop. It's that time."

Craggy mountains, blue-black with shadow, margined the shoreline. He saw a cove shrouded with dark-green growth, very tropical looking. He crawled back and relieved Polly at the tiller. Soon the outlines of the cove became clear. It was about a half-mile deep, with a white beach backing it up. Dense mangrove thickets fringed the beach. As they neared a landing, they discovered the entrance to another cove hidden behind the main one. On the spit between the coves there was coarse sand and a mangrove thicket. They beached the boat and Eric built a fire. Small black gnats infested the area, not stinging but troublesome.

"We forgot to fish," Eric pointed out. "What's for dinner?"

"Canned stew and fruit. Hey!" Polly was staring at the shallow inner cove. "That looks like clam country. I think Dad and I clammed here last year. I *know* we did."

While the food heated, they waded in a foot of water, raking their fingers through the wet sand. Immediately they began dredging up rough-shelled butter clams the size of silver dollars. Polly steamed them in one of Eric's cooking pots. They were working now by firelight. She melted oleo and drained the salt water off the clams. The shells gaped; with forks they extracted the clams, dipped them in oleo, and gulped them down. Grease shone on their chins as they ate. Eric would never have eaten them at home, yet they were delicious.

They washed everything and unrolled sleeping gear. "Boys to the right, girls to the left," Polly said. She walked into the darkness beyond the boat. He heard her spreading her blankets on the sand, then blowing up an air mattress. Night had flooded the cove with a tide of darkness. The gnats had disappeared, but a few mosquitoes sang around Eric's head. In the mangrove swamp, rock oysters were popping open with sharp explosive sounds. A fox yipped on a ridge.

"Want some help?" he called.

"Well—do you mind? I'm getting winded."

Sitting on the sand, they took turns at inflating the air mattress. When Eric's knee touched her thigh, he could almost hear a crack of electricity; both of them started.

He was thinking about how the sexes found each other. Only two human beings in twenty-five miles tonight, and here they were, inches apart. Birds nestling together, dolphins pairing off, coyotes buddying up in their dens. Two by two. Great old system of nature's. He was breathless, only partly from blowing on the valve stem of the mattress.

"That's fine," Polly said. "Thanks a lot. Good night, now."

"Polly . . ." Eric began.

"Good night!" Polly said, giving him a push.

"Okay! I was just going to say that I've never known any girl like you. I mean it. Yesterday, on the beach, I had this feeling—better get out while you can, fella . . ."

Polly slapped a mosquito. "Gee, I hope we're not going to have mosquitoes," she said.

"Use your judo on them," Eric said, making a judo chop.

"I'm saving that for you."

Eric felt like a boiler whose seams were being tested. He had things to say that would not keep. He would lie there all night. Because the enormous fact was that he thought he was falling in love with her. It seemed very important to him that she realize that.

"A good-night kiss wouldn't hurt, would it?" he said.

She gave him another push. "Good night!"

Eric held her wrist. "I mean it, Polly. You're a very special job."

Polly sighed. "Eric, am I going to have to walk back?"

Eric dropped her hand. "Okay! Blow up your own mattress after this, blonde."

"Believe me!" Polly said.

He walked away and smoothed a patch of sand with the blade of a paddle. He spread his sleeping bag and slid into it. He lay there feeling as though he might be coming down with the flu. She was right, though; the situation was risky, at best. The civilized man's burden. I wonder who worked out this system? Some cat about ninety, I'll bet.

He had been in bed only a few minutes when Polly called out in a loud whisper, "Eric? I hear something!"

"That's me panting," Eric muttered.

"I think it's a snake rattling! It's coming toward my head."

Eric scrambled from his sleeping bag and groped around for his spear gun. "Don't move! I'll be right there." He found his flashlight, cocked the spear gun, and tiptoed toward where she lay.

"Behind me!" she whispered.

A couple of yards from her head he saw something on the sand: a crooked mangrove branch. He searched, but found nothing else other than a few crabs at the water line. Uncocking the gun, he gazed at her as she lay still in her sleeping bag.

Good show, blonde, he thought. Anything to keep me stirred up, eh?

There was another possibility. Perhaps what she had really been saying was, *I've changed my mind about that kiss.* Because the truth was, a crab didn't make sounds anything like a rattlesnake.

He knelt on one knee beside her. "You've got one of those wild imaginations," he said, grinning. "There were only a few crabs and a stick."

He could see her face clearly in the moonlight. Big-eyed, she gazed up at him. "I'm sorry. I'm a nuisance, aren't I?"

He leaned over her. "A kiss and all is forgiven."

Polly's hands came between them, pushing vigorously at his chest. "No, Eric. Nothing physical—I can't handle it."

He sat back, baffled. "Where'd you read that—on a fortune card from a weighing machine? Can't *handle* it?"

"Go away. I mean, I can't handle anything physical. I—I don't know, I just—I really did think it was a snake, Eric. I wasn't teasing."

"You can't handle what?" Eric jeered.

"Well—physical contact. I don't know how I'd react."

Eric sighed and looked down at her in disgust. There was no doubt in his mind that she had staged the whole show. But why, if she hadn't intended to go through with it? Grimacing, he pointed the spear gun at her, then gave a snort. Getting to his feet, he plodded back to the boy's area.

"Hey, Captain!" Polly called. "I'm sorry."

Eric grunted.

"You see, the situation is bigger than either of us, and I don't want it to get out of hand."

"What are you doing now, pulling off the scab to make sure

I'm not healing? I'll leave the spear gun here, if you need it. I'm going for a walk. Yell if you need help."

"Why don't you just settle down? Think about cool green fields . . ."

Eric walked up the sand a couple of hundred yards. He stepped on a sharp shell and had to sit down and rub his heel. He lay on the sand gazing up at the black velvet of the night. A bright object moved into his vision, too fast for a plane, too long-lived for a shooting star. A satellite? He watched it travel evenly across the cloudy emptiness of the Milky Way. After it vanished, he headed back.

"Gee, I was scared," Polly said, when he returned.

"You might as well shut up," Eric said. "I feel fine now."

"I'm so glad! It's all in your mind, actually."

Keep talking, Eric thought. You'll wind up walking back yet.

chapter **19**

Eric's first impression in the morning was of Polly sitting on the edge of the canoe brushing her hair. Long and golden, it ran with the lavender light of dawn. She looked like a beached mermaid. A small fire was burning. He sniffed coffee and discovered a tin cup beside his sleeping bag.

"Let's get this show on the road, Captain," Polly called.

Eric sat up cross-legged and sipped the coffee. He felt purged of his madness of last night. He sniffed again. Bacon!

"How long have you been up?"

"Hours. Breakfast will be ready after you wash up."

Since nothing would keep long without ice, they consumed

a pound of bacon, a papaya, and four eggs. Eric stowed gear and rolled his sleeping bag. He doubled up a piece of bacon and baited his hand line. A breeze riffled the sail.

He looked for Polly. He had thought she might want privacy, so he had not tried to keep track of her. She was sitting on the sand near the mangroves brushing her hair again.

"How 'bout it?" he called. "All lines singled up."

Polly waved the brush. "Just a minute!" After a few more strokes she came to the boat. "If I don't keep up with it," she said, "it gets so tangled it's like something the cat's played with. Do you know how to braid hair?" she asked.

Eric rubbed a mosquito bite on his neck. "I don't get many calls, so I'm out of practice. But—"

Polly handed him the brush. "If you'll start it for me, I can finish up in the boat."

He was anxious to be off, but she was such a good sport about everything . . . "I'll try," he said.

It was easy and relaxing, like occupational therapy. *Over, under, under, over.* Her hair was like silk.

"That's fine," she said, after he had braided about a foot for her.

Since she wore slacks today, having got a slight sunburn yesterday, Eric had her sit in the bow while he pushed the boat into deeper water. Polly sat braiding her hair. The hull ground in the sand. As he pushed, his feet sank into the bottom. He was soaked to the waist before the canoe floated free. Polly did not offer to help.

After fifteen minutes, they were clear of the land and course was set for the next point south.

"Where's this pearl-oyster bed you were telling me about?" he asked.

The canoe was rocking along past a jagged range of black lunar hills.

"We might be there by tonight," Polly said.

"Is it really that great?"

She smiled, though somehow not so warmly as she had earlier. "Yes, it's beautiful."

"Hey, blonde!"

She glanced back, her paddle raised and dripping. The breeze had lightened and they were augmenting sailpower with the paddles.

"What?"

"Level with me. Do you wear contacts?"

"What makes you think I do?"

"Something about the way you look at me. Near-sighted girls have a sort of happy, confused look."

"Yes, I do," she said. She looked down, shyly.

"I never see you take them out. Don't you have to every so often?"

"Yes, but it only takes a second. I'm shy about it."

"Do they bother you?"

"Sometimes. When it's smoggy my eyes smart."

"I should think they'd protect your eyes against smog."

She smiled but made no reply. He felt stupid. *I guess that was a stupid thing to say,* he thought. He was not sure why.

He brightened. "I read once that some cowboy actor's horse had one blue eye and one brown eye, and it had to wear a colored contact lens so they'd both be the same color. It sounds kind of far-fetched . . ." he admitted, lamely.

Polly gazed at the shore without replying. Her silence gave him to understand that the remark had been in bad taste, like telling a racial joke. He quit talking.

"You might as well throw out the hand line and troll," Eric said. They had eaten lunch on the wing. Polly let the hand line down and a few minutes later a fish struck. While Eric cleaned the fish, Polly scrutinized the shore. The hills were like purplish-brown slag.

"I remember this spot," she said. "Dad and I camped here. There's a better beach around the next point, though. That's where we got the pearl oysters."

A few minutes later they sailed around a point and entered a blue-green cove like a pirate's anchorage. Steep bluffs enclosed a gleaming scallop of water. The small beach was clean and white. At one point a cluster of palm trees grew from the rocks near the water.

Polly gazed overside. "It's clear as crystal! You can see the bottom."

Far down, Eric made out sand, rocks, and weed. "How deep did you find the shells?" he asked.

"The ones we found were only a few feet down."

"Let's make camp and then eyeball it."

Fifteen or twenty yards offshore, Polly laid her paddle aside. "I might as well take my contacts out now," she said. "I don't like to swim with them on."

Modestly, she averted her face during the operation. Why? Eric wondered. Was it like removing one's dentures?

Resting her elbow on the gunwale, Polly bent her head forward. Suddenly she made a grasping gesture and cried out.

"My lenses!"

Eric nearly dropped his paddle. "What? What happened?"

"I dropped my contacts overboard!"

"Drop the anchor!" Eric yelled. He snatched up the wire-bound rock that served as a stern anchor and heaved it into the water, watching it go down in a cloud of bubbles. The water was only twelve or fifteen feet deep. But how did one find something transparent in the water?

On hands and knees, Polly was groping about in the bilge. "I can't see the anchor! Oh, Eric . . ."

Stunned with the knowledge of her loss, Eric crawled forward to pick up the anchor and hurl it overboard. *My gosh, she's practically blind!* he thought. He scrambled back, found his face mask, and leaned over the gunwale to press the glass plate against the water, making a porthole through which to view the bottom.

"We'll find 'em," he told Polly staunchly as she sat helplessly on the thwart.

The bottom beneath the boat resembled a relief map, a smooth stone plateau split by miniature canyons and patches of sand where lacy sargassum weed grew in tawny clusters. And where, in all that shifting seascape, were the two crystal cockles that enabled a girl who could not even find an anchor without them to read fine print?

"I'm going to put on my trunks," he said.

Polly turned away, a mere concession to formality since doubtless she could barely see him anyway. He pulled on face mask and fins, took the snorkel in his teeth, and slipped overside. Face down, he studied the bottom. He knew that fish tended to cluster about anything that dropped into the water. But could they see glass any better than he? Swarms of yellow and black sergeant majors were nibbling at his anchors. Others, in purple and yellow stripes, cruised aimlessly back and forth. A porcupine fish, alarmed by the excitement, inflated itself like a thorny football. No clues among the fish, he decided.

Though knowing the search was hopeless, he submerged into the cool silence. Selecting a sandy area, he began patting his hands against the bottom, feeling futile and foolish. In a minute or so he was forced to surface. Panting, he watched Polly near-sightedly squinting at him. She smiled bravely and waved.

On the second dive, just as he was running out of air, he saw a bed of rough-shelled oysters anchored to some rocks. He worked a couple off, carried them up, and dropped them in the boat.

"How big are the lenses?" he panted.

"Oh, about—" With her thumb and forefinger, Polly made a little ring. Suddenly she tipped her head back and laughed. "Oh, Eric! You're so funny."

Eric pawed his nose to see whether it was running, the likeliest comic situation he could think of. "What's funny?" he asked her.

"You are. Did you really think I wore contacts? I was just teasing . . . !" She put both hands over her mouth and giggled. "I couldn't resist!"

Eric thought about revenge. Tip the boat over. Drag her out. Splash her. He drew his hand back to hurl water over her. She screamed. He restrained himself, hating to ruin her nice white slacks and red blouse. At the same time, he knew where nice guys finished.

"The last of the old-time comics," he said.

He groped in the boat for a screwdriver, then recharged his lungs and dived. Crazy girl. Not that it was serious; it was just that he wouldn't have done it to her. Who wanted to be made a fool of? Maybe Dr. Nestor wasn't so dumb, dumping her on him.

He collected some more oysters and surfaced with them. Polly had removed her blouse; under her clothing she wore a two-piece swimsuit. She called contritely:

"Eric!"

He stuck his thumbs in his ears, waggled his fingers at her, and dived again.

Long before dark they had a bucket full of pearl oysters. They made camp, then set about opening the shells with the small machete and an abalone iron. Opening a marl-encrusted shell to find a softly shining interior was a breathtaking surprise. The shells ran with pearly nacre, colorful as a film of oil on water. But in a half-hour's work they discovered only one tiny pearl the size of a peppercorn.

Eric presented it to Polly. "When this you see, remember me. And it will serve you right."

She laughed. The sky was now rich with color; a single long shadow sprawled out from a cliff to darken the entire cove. The cove was as still and cool as if underwater. Polly put her hand on his arm.

"Will you get the fire going and start the fish?" she said. "There's a little spring down where those palms are. I want to rinse the salt out of my hair. It gets just like a bath mat if I don't wash it every day."

She picked up a towel and strolled off. Irritated, Eric started hunting driftwood. Keep it up, he thought. I'll trade you in on a squaw before we get halfway there. What had changed her? His kissing her the other day? Trying to kiss her last night? Or just the smell of infatuation on him? To a girl, that might be like a boxer's dropping his guard. The idea here seemed to be to hit him with everything but the water bucket.

chapter **20**

Gear had been stowed and the morning tide was drifting south. In the sky a few pink clouds floated like wisps of incandescent vapor. Already it was hot. Eric washed the dishes while Polly folded and repacked her clothing. Standing ankle-deep in the water, he watched her, covertly. Though she worked quickly, she seemed to get nothing done. She would fold a garment and lay it in her little sea bag; then start to pack her hairbrush but decide to give her hair a few more strokes. Then she had to take everything out to locate a pair of sandals. Yet all was done with verve and interest, as though packing were some exciting game.

She waved at him. "Almost ready!"

He wished he could get the point across to her that, while the trip appeared to be a matter of fun, it was actually a race.

"My, it's hot!"

Sitting in the bow, Polly tried to stay in the shade of the jib. She had swum for a while, then spread her hair into a tent over her shoulders to dry. A spiritless breeze teased the sails.

"It's even hotter," Eric said, "when you're paddling."

Polly took up her paddle. "Why didn't you tell me you wanted me to paddle?" she said petulantly. "How was I supposed to know?"

"I'm telling you now."

Kneeling, Polly began to paddle. Big production of each stroke—such hard work—interfering with her hair drying, etc. Now she's got her feelings hurt, Eric thought.

Almost lunchtime. A good breeze ballooned the sails. *Delfina* rolled through the water like a porpoise. Polly was reading a book. Eric's empty stomach was caving in.

"How about some chow?" he said.

"Just a minute—I want to finish this page. Or you can open a can of fruit and get out the rolls and peanut butter."

"Okay. But they're under your seat."

"Oh—I'm sorry."

She handed the lunch things back to him. Brief smile, back to reading. Eric broke open a roll. Then he frowned. No knife.

"How about a knife?" he said. "And the can opener."

"Oh—sorry."

Through the afternoon a succession of clamshell bays marched by, rimmed by ceramic desert hills. Polly swam again; then Eric swam, heat-dazed. The water restored him to vigor. He baited and set the hand line. Just after he had relieved Polly at the tiller, a fish struck hard. It sounded, rose to splash along the surface, then dived again; suddenly the line went dead, but a weight lay at the end of it. Eric brought the fish in hand over hand. Under the boat he saw it, chunky and not very long.

"Big fight for a little fish," he said, puzzled.

At that instant a huge torpedo shape rolled up; in one pass, it devoured the hooked fish. Eric shouted and took a turn of the line about a cleat. The big fish itself was now hooked.

"Shark!" he yelled.

The sudden tug had come when the shark chewed off half the hooked fish. The shark now went deep. The heavy monofilament line stretched, sang, parted like a cobweb. Eric shuddered.

"Hate those things!" he said through his teeth.

"Are you *sure* it was a shark?" Seeming amused, Polly turned her head on the side, quizzically.

"Positive."

"They're good eating, you know."

"Fine. Catch me one."

"Aren't you going to troll?" Polly's eyes were large and innocent.

"With him hanging around? Nuts to that."

"I don't think he'd strike, not with a hook in his throat. If he did, you could horse him in with gloves and then harpoon him."

"The thought drives me back," Eric said, clutching the tiller.

Polly smiled with some private amusement. In anger, Eric blurted:

"Yeah, what?"

"Nothing. Only a boy who was down here last year got a *huge* shark that way. . . ."

Eric's will set like cement. The accusation was clear: the other boy had guts. He baited a hook and tossed it out, a large and rusty hook that even a shark could not straighten.

"Satisfied?" he asked.

She shrugged and turned forward. He could not keep his eyes off the line. Scarcely had the boat gained way when a long, solid yank lifted the line in gleaming rings from the floor. He knew for sure that he had hooked into a big one.

His arms and shoulders ached with fighting it. Polly clapped each time he began hauling the big fish in. But always it staged a run that left him exhausted. He braced himself against a sudden, heavy series of tugs; a moment later the line went slack. But when he began retrieving the line, a slow, stubborn pull set in. At last he saw it—a long shape rising slowly in a cloud of blood like pink smoke.

He was cold with a sudden prevision of what was to come. The shark had been torn by another shark. The other shark must be following. As he reached for a knife to cut the line, a shark-shadow glided up from under the boat and began to mangle the wounded shark; then a third shark lunged in. Eric felt their bodies jarring the keel.

Polly screamed. "Cut the line! Cut the line!"

"Where's the knife?" Eric yelled. He took a bight over a cleat, then realized that a sudden pull before he cut the line would overturn the canoe. *Oh, you crazy dame! Where's the knife? Where is the knife?* There it was—lying smeared with peanut butter where Polly had left it. With a quick slash, he severed the nylon filament close to the boat.

He seized the harpoon and jabbed the point against the bleeding shark to force it away from the boat. "Paddle!" he yelled. Polly snatched up a paddle, but lost it overside with her first panicky stroke. Eric retrieved it from the bloody water and shoved it back at her. He hauled in the sail. The heavy hull lay dead in the water. At least three sharks were tearing at the dying one, rocking the boat with their struggles.

At last the boat began to move. A shark struck the paddle and tore it from his grasp. He clutched at it as it was floating away and rethreaded it through the rope ring at the stern. Gasping, he worked the oar back and forth, sculling for extra speed. Finally Polly cried,

"We're all right! They're 'way behind us."

Eric stared at her, winded and pale. "For a nickel," he said, "I'd throw you to them right now."

Polly looked hurt. "What do you mean?"

"You needled me into that! You nearly finished us! Admit it."

Polly hung her head, her eyes filling. "I'm sorry. I didn't think anything like that would happen."

"You'd better do more paddling and less horsing around," Eric snapped. "I can get deckhands like you off any Hallowe'en broomstick."

"I'm sorry," Polly said again, keeping her head down. "I'm awfully sorry."

"Keep horsing around. Keep needling. Next time I'll put you ashore."

Polly faced forward and began paddling. "I'm sorry," she repeated humbly.

"The life you save may be your own," Eric said. "You dumb dame."

They beached the boat early. He cast from a rock in the water and caught a pargo. While he fished, Polly built a fire and unpacked everything. She put pans of food to heat and was waiting with a fish knife to clean the pargo.

"Let me," she said. "I'm pretty good at it."

Kneeling on the sand, she deftly fileted the snapper. With her head bowed and her braid hanging down her back, she looked like a young peasant woman. In fact, he guessed, it was the part she was currently playing at their neighborhood theatre. Not long ago she had been the White Queen; then it was the spoiled Girl Sailor of the *Delfina*. Now she was the Contrite Muchacha. If a man got permanently tangled with her, which would turn out to be the part she played seven days a week? Maybe that would depend on him.

She fried the fish, served the food, and made sure Eric had everything before she herself took a bite. It was all very little-theatre. *Next thing,* Eric thought, *she'll be washing my back.* She ate a few bites, then said thoughtfully,

"I'm a witch."

"Why?"

"I *was* being nasty."

"How come?"

". . . I don't know. Girls just do those things, I guess. We're really not aware of doing them, actually."

"Even old girls like my mother," Eric said. "If she hadn't torpedoed my father's idea to buy a garage, he might not have taken off."

"And then you wouldn't have met me and had such an awful time," Polly said.

Eric started to blurt out, *Oh, I didn't mean that! I like you when you're behaving yourself, etc.* But he decided to play a part, too—the Viking Warrior with his woman.

"Breaks," he said. "Pass me another roll, will you?"

The night was so warm that he lay for some time on top of his sleeping bag before crawling in. Guilt assailed him. The terse truth was that he was as guilty in the near disaster as was

Polly. For he had known it was risky to throw out the hook; yet he had done it. It did not matter *why* he had done it: in fact, he had done it knowing he would probably hook into trouble. The point was that he was in a very special position, now. Like a sea captain, he was responsible for everything that happened to them. There was no one else to blame. It was of the greatest importance, therefore, to make decisions carefully and hang with them. He recalled how Gregorio and Angel had never responded immediately to anything he said. He had assumed that they were merely slow-thinking peasants. The fact was they were thinking instead of chattering. When one of them said, *Yes, I will,* or *No, I won't,* or *Be careful,* he meant it. After a while, he thought, such decision-making might become instinctive, the problem and the decision welded together.

One thing was sure: a girl would have little to say about how a *vagabundo* ran his boat. She would have to play her theatrics somewhere else.

chapter 21

Playing a modified Peasant Girl role, Polly served a very acceptable breakfast. The modification consisted of a secret confidence, as though she had information that tomorrow the voting requirements would be lowered to include peasants such as she. Eric minded his business but kept a cold eye on her. After eating, he said,

"I'm going to wash the crud out of the boat. We'll leave in fifteen minutes."

Polly bit her lip in doubt. She had spread on bushes garments dampened in the bilge during yesterday's excitement. They were not all dry yet.

"I'll try to be ready," she said doubtfully.

But in fifteen minutes she was still hurrying from bush to

bush, turning one garment to catch the sun more directly, shaking another and rehanging it.

Eric, squeezing a sponge beside the boat, called, "Five minutes!"

"I'm almost ready! Wait for me!"

With all gear stowed, he looked once more at his watch. Twenty-five minutes had passed since his first warning. Thoughtfully he studied Polly's back as she neatly placed things in the red sea bag. Two blouses and a pair of white capris were still drying. Like an automatic reel, she immediately took up any slack he allowed. She was perfectly amazing. She had not learned a thing yesterday.

He rolled his pants legs and pushed the boat into a foot of crystal water. Then he stepped in, seated himself, and raised his paddle. The hull crisply broke the water and the paddle created a deep, strong bubbling. Without a backward look, he stroked away—dip, pull, twist the paddle; dip, pull, twist. His back and shoulder muscles had strengthened. He felt them working painlessly as the paddle slashed the green flesh of the water.

"Eric!"

He never turned his head.

"Eric, come back!"

He continued to paddle while the wailing persisted. The time came to set the sails. He fixed the jib, crawled back and set the mainsheet. For several minutes he heard her calling. After about fifteen minutes he glanced back and saw a small figure trudging down the beach with a red sack on its shoulder.

After two hours he beached the boat. He might lose a little time today, but he would unquestionably make it up later in nuisance-time saved. He snorkeled around for a while, seeing nothing very interesting. A very large yellow sea worm, or a very small yellow snake, burrowed into the sand under him. Then a vivid orange nudibranch, lost from some rocky area, swam by with the aimless motions of a butterfly. He captured it, but on his palm it collapsed into a little puddle of jelly. Released, it fluttered off on its mysterious mission.

He spread a towel to lie on. The immaculate sand was engraved with the cuneiform tracks of shore birds. Above him the sun glowed like heated iron; but the breeze was cool with the hiss of sea water. Peace and relaxation dropped him: he slept.

"It was *wrong! Anything* could have happened to me! My father will be furious!"

He had awakened as she approached the boat. Yawning, he trickled sand through his fist, letting her rage. With the red bag lying before her, she stood flushed and perspiring, her hair straggling over her face.

"Someone might have attacked me! And my shoulders—! They're absolutely raw from carrying this darned thing. My father—"

"The last thing your father told me was, 'Defend yourself at all times.' Do you want to eat before we go on?"

Polly planted her fists on her hips and glared at him. She kicked some sand over him. She walked over to the boat and kicked it. Then she stepped into the boat, pulled some things from under the tarp, and came back.

"We might as well eat now," she said sulkily.

A few minutes after they set sail, she said, "I guess I'd better put the line out, hadn't I?"

"Might as well," Eric told her.

By that night, according to Polly's figuring, they were an easy day's cruise from Bahía Escondida. In the distance a chain of islands rested on the water. Just beyond them, she said, lay Bahía Escondida—the Hidden Bay.

During the night, Eric awoke to hear sand peppering his sleeping bag. A strong wind had sprung up. He sat up, anxious about the boat. The black sky was punctured with stars; the waves came running in one after another to fall heavily on the beach. In shorts, he plodded down to the water. The boat had turned broadside to the waves in shallow water; the larger waves were breaking over it. He worked the stern into deeper water. Incoming waves urged the boat up the sand. Eric pushed. Finally he set the stern anchor, then moved the bow anchor farther up the sand.

Shivering, he wormed back into his blankets. The sand stung his face and he pulled his head inside.

By morning the wind was stronger still and the water was rough and dirty. They stood looking at the expanse of whitecaps.

"How long does it usually blow?" Eric asked.

"Usually only a day or so. I suppose we could cruise close to shore and paddle—"

"We'd get dumped," Eric predicted. "We'll have to wait till it dies down."

The wind blew strongly all day. Despite the breeze, the sun was hot. Eric erected a canvas shelter, but it kept blowing down. They explored the slaglike foothills, found a small cave, and dug for Indian artifacts. Under ancient dust and silt they found a few small stone scrapers.

"You know how poor these Indians were?" Eric said. "When they got a piece of meat, they'd tie a thong to it, and the guy that won the toss would chew and swallow it. Then he'd pull it up again and pass it along."

"If you know any more Indian lore," Polly said, "don't tell me."

"That's nothing," Eric said. "Lemme tell you what they did with fish guts . . ."

Polly covered her ears.

The day was a howler right up to dark. A couple of fishing boats passed at a distance, lunging through the short troughs like motorcycles going over a plowed field. Spray flew. But after dark the wind gradually died. With the silence, his tension relaxed. He had been unconsciously braced against the howl of wind and the sting of sand.

In a still, hot morning they paddled for hours. But the islands they had sighted before the big blow kept their distance. Flushed and wispy-haired, Polly licked a finger and raised it.

"Wind's coming up!" she said.

Soon they were heeling along in a good breeze.

The first of the islands lay on the water like a sleeping lion, its head to the north. "That's Pichilingue," Polly cried happily. "It means 'pirate.' Some buccaneer is supposed to have holed up here. The main thing it's got, according to an old man who lives there, is sharks."

"What's he live on?" Pichilingue looked like a typical Baja island, a heap of stones populated by birds and insects.

"Sharks and pearls, I think. He doesn't talk much. He comes to Dad to have his teeth cleaned. Just a status thing, Dad says, to prove he can afford it. He doesn't have one single cavity, and he's about a hundred years old."

As they passed the island, a small sailboat floated from behind it, a *panga* like their own.

"I'll bet that's Lázaro, the old man," Polly said. "He's going to town."

The boats drew together. "Don't try to talk to him," Polly warned, "unless he starts it. He's a real hermit type. They say he kills sharks with a knife, just for thrills."

"And he's a hundred years old?"

"Well, maybe seventy."

When the boats were about twenty yards apart, the old man raised one arm in greeting. That was all. Eric had a glimpse of a brown-skinned old man with a short, bristly white beard and spiky hair. He wore a patched blue shirt and dungarees. Then the old man moved so that he was behind the sail and out of sight. Since his boat was more lightly loaded, he had soon drawn far ahead.

About noon they sailed past a high, dark headland. Polly splashed water on Eric.

"Whee! We made it! I, Polly Nestor, claim this bay for the City of San Francisco."

Eric was numbed by the contrast of the beautiful bay before them with the lunar desert they had come through. Between two dark headlands lay a half-circle of blue water. A long sickle of sand set into the apex of the bay was divided by a river flowing from a little valley choked with trees. Eric could not see the town, but smoke rose from the trees upriver.

Polly began orating like the man with the megaphone on a sightseeing bus.

"The town's up the river a mile or so. Dad camps near the church. It's about halfway to town—there aren't so many mosquitoes there. They fish for turtles and shrimp out of here. That looks like Captain Gallardo's boat, doesn't it? Dad says if he ever scrapes off the rust the boat will fall apart."

One shrimper looked about like another, but the boat anchored near the river mouth did appear rustier than most. Two other boats rode at anchor in the bay. Eric searched the beach for a yellow canoe, while Polly chattered on.

"I wonder if we beat Dad? He was going to make a stop. We'll have to paddle up the river before we can see anything. That bright green is sugar cane, the darker green is corn. They have papayas as big as footballs here!"

Despite her happy prattling, gloom hung on Eric like an old sweatshirt. After all the paddling, the shark-fighting, the hoping, the struggle to catch up, he was convinced he had missed him again. Polly saw his disappointment and said, with a hand-squeeze:

"Cheer up! He wouldn't camp on the beach anyway with so many nice campsites along the river. It's an amazing river! Simply bursts out of the hills a few miles away, and everywhere it passes the people have crops and animals and good clothes."

Somberly Eric adjusted course. "You want to know how it is with El Rojo?" he said. "He fixed somebody's washing machine here four days ago, passed out pliers, and took off for the next collection of broken-down machinery to the south. And when they find out who I am, they'll say, 'Yankee, go home!' "

Polly's laugh tinkled. She was full of joy at arriving: *Role #6: Gabby Sun-Tanned Girl Back from Camp.*

They skimmed across the bay and paddled up the river. There were irrigated fields and clearings where adobe huts stood, festooned with vines and scarlet bougainvillaea. Burros and bicycles moved along a road on the north bank. They paddled along like aborigines on a jungle river. On the north bank, ten minutes upriver, they came upon a very old church, a mere block of whitewashed masonry among giant mango trees. A low adobe wall enclosed it, whitewashed once, now crusted with brown plaster like a hog with mud. Just visible above the wall were blackened stone grave markers.

"Head for that ditch," Polly said. "We can pull in there."

The outfall of an irrigation ditch had cut a wedge into the riverbank, grotesque roots crisscrossing the aperture. Polly tied up to one of the roots, jumped out and stretched. Eric sat limply.

"Dad isn't here yet," Polly said, surveying the campsite by the church wall. "We beat him!"

"Very classy campsite," Eric commented. "When you get tired of counting gravestones, you can be a pallbearer in a funeral."

Laughing, Polly started along a trail to a clearing. Eric shouldered a sack of gear and plodded along the cemetery wall behind her. He stopped dead on seeing a bright blue cross beside the path. The soil was freshly turned, wreaths of paper flowers hanging on the cross. His stomach turned over. On the crossbar were painted in white the words:

EL GRINGO

Something about this marker outside the wall chilled him. "What's that thing doing out here?" he asked.

Polly lowered her sea bag. "A new grave!"

"How come it's not inside the cemetery?"

"Well, it says 'El Gringo'—the American—so maybe the person who died wasn't a Catholic. Therefore he couldn't be buried in sacred ground."

The cold crept into Eric's heart like frost. "Are you sure you never saw it before?"

"Yes, but it *may* have been there all the time. See, they've been clearing away the weeds."

"But the mound is fresh," Eric pointed out.

Polly approached the cross and knelt by it. "There's no date on it. Hmm. Over on the Pacific side there's a grave that says, 'Here Lies a Vagabundo of the Sea,' and there are *three* crosses on it. Strangers die, and the people bury them and tend the graves——"

Eric set the bag of supplies on the ground. He was trembling. "Polly, I've got to talk to somebody in town about this. Or maybe there's a priest . . ."

"No, the padre only comes once a month. It *couldn't* be your——be him——"

Eric sagged onto the sea bag. "He was a lousy sailor, even when we had a cabin cruiser," he said. "The Coast Guard always had to tow us back. He wouldn't have had sense enough to wait out that wind yesterday. He probably paddled right into the middle of it."

A big man in dungarees and a dirty tee shirt strolled from the church. He set a black engineer's cap on the back of his head. Something about the man plucked at Eric's sleeve. The Mexican picked up the stub of a cigar from where it rested on a pink granite cross and lighted it. As he dropped the match, his glance linked with Eric's.

In silence and shock they stared at each other.

"Captain Gallardo!" Eric called.

"Yes, hello. Very nice to see you," called the captain. "I am glad the big wind did not finish you. Well, I've got to go in town now and pay my men——"

"Wait!"

Eric vaulted the wall into the churchyard. Captain Gallardo, who had recently shaved, smelled richly of bay rum. Under his skin his whiskers were so black that his jaw looked as though it had been hammered out of iron.

"There's a cross out there——" Eric said, nervously.

"Yes. I don't know anything about it. You'd better ask someone in town—Fernando León, for instance, the mayor."

"But . . . ?"

"The people say a gringo washed up on the beach. That's all I know."

Eric gripped his wrist. "I'll pay you to dig it up! I've got to be sure. Then I want to radio my mother again."

"You'll have to have a paper from Hilario Conseco, the Federal policeman, before you can dig. I wouldn't worry, there are other *vagabundos*—"

"Gringo *vagabundos*?"

Captain Gallardo puffed intently on the cigar; but, in the end, had to relight it. After a few acrid puffs he said,

"Weep over nothing until it has happened. I'll take you to Fernando, the *delegado*."

chapter **22**

Eric paced the main street of Bahía Escondida with Captain Gallardo. In this primitive setting the town had the look of a metropolis, though it consisted principally of a narrow cobbled street paralleling the river, with small side streets wandering off into the thickets. High plastered walls and the blank façades of buildings walled the road on both sides. Beside the walks grew huge old laurel trees, their trunks whitewashed and their leaves dusty. Through open doors Eric glimpsed courtyards of sprinkled earth crowded with tropical plants.

The clatter of a telegraph key came like the tapping of a distant woodpecker.

"Good! The *delegado* is in his office," said the captain. "Fernando is also the telegrapher."

He turned in at a small corner office. Within the dusky interior a backless bench stood against a wall; behind a wooden railing was a desk littered with papers. A big, paunchy man in a white shirt sat at the desk. He wore thick glasses and his forehead was marred by a scar. The key continued clicking as he rose to give Captain Gallardo the *abrazo*. He was perspiring, and, as Captain Gallardo introduced Eric, his free hand dabbed at his brow with a wadded handkerchief.

"About the grave of that *vagabundo*, Fernando," said the fisherman. "This *joven* is, well, quite anxious."

"You see," Eric blurted, "there's a chance that—"

"Yes, I know. I can't tell you much except that the gringo floated in during the big wind. Some fishermen found him on the beach and buried him."

Eric, his knees going weak, slumped onto the bench.

After a moment he asked, "Did you save the papers and things in his clothes?"

"There were no papers. Nothing."

"What color was his hair?"

Fernando lifted his shoulders to signify, *Don't know*.

"Can I telegraph from here to San Diego?" Eric asked.

"No. Only to Santa Rosalía and Mulegé."

Eric started to speak, but his throat dried and he had to clear it several times before he could make a sound.

"I'll have to make sure whether it's my father or not, Mayor. I'll have to dig . . ."

Again the mayor patted his moist brow. His spectacles were so greasy that Eric wondered how he saw through them.

"Understood. But you'll have to do it tomorrow. A paper is required from the Federal authorities. Captain Conseco is the

Federal policeman here, and he has driven down the beach to supervise the loading of some cattle onto a boat."

"When will he be back?"

"Late. *Ah, míre!*" said the mayor, beaming. "We have talked about this. The people feel very badly and want to hold a *velorio* for you near the church. To take your mind—"

"What's a *velorio?*" Eric asked, edgily.

"A wake," murmured Captain Gallardo.

"Food, drink, good companions for a few hours! It makes it easier. A custom of ours, an old one, from the very heart."

"I have a turtle aboard," said the shrimp captain quickly. "My cook will prepare it. All the big people in town will be there, young Hansen. Tequila, beer, food for everyone!"

Eric nodded gloomily. "Okay. But what if it isn't him?"

"Ah, in that case," said the mayor, patting his glistening brow and smiling, "it will be a celebration! In any event, it will not cost you a centavo, and will start at noon tomorrow!"

When they emerged, Eric saw a familiar figure walking up the middle of the road carrying a parcel: Lázaro, the shark fisherman. He was alone and did not look as though he belonged in Bahía Escondida. He appeared solitary and proud, like a fearless man roaming a hostile town.

At the camp, Polly was removing the meat from a pair of lobsters a fisherman had given her. "It probably means he needs an inlay and can't pay for it," she said. "Can you eat as early as this? It's only four."

Eric muttered agreement. He sat on his bedroll, gazing at the whitewashed church and at the gravestones huddled before it.

Polly hurried to serve dinner. She melted oleo to dip the lobster meat in. It was sweet and tender, and until he looked at the grave again Eric ate with good appetite. But when it came home to him that there was every reason to believe that his father lay in the ground there, he laid aside his mess kit and walked down to the river.

During the night Dr. Nestor drove in. It was still early. Living outdoors, one got in the habit of going to bed with the birds. The camper backed in with a snapping of underbrush and a growling of gears, then went quiet.

Eric heard Polly say, "Hi, Dad."

"Hello, dear. Everything go all right?"

"Tell you in the morning."

"That's a mysterious statement if I ever heard one."

"Good night, Pops," Polly said.

Dr. Nestor had already been told about the grave, it developed. As they breakfasted, he said: "I wouldn't worry about it, Eric. Frankly, I think there's something fishy."

"Why?"

"There are too many signs around that your father was here —alive. Someone repaired the refrigerator in Sanchez's *cantina*. He wouldn't tell me who. Said he did it himself. Rubbish! Sanchez can hardly get the cap off a beer bottle without calling in a mechanic. Also I found Fernando *typing* a message instead of writing it longhand. His typewriter's been fixed!"

Eric said, "Huh!"

"I don't think they'd be so cruel," said Polly.

"Have you ever seen them kill a turtle?" said her father. "If the situation calls for cruelty, they're as capable of it as anyone."

While they ate, people had begun to collect before the church and on the road. Most of them were dressed as if for a holiday. They stood around waiting patiently. Three of Captain Gallardo's men rowed up the river in a dinghy and brought ashore the two halves of a turtle shell. They propped the sections upright on the ground facing each other and built a fire between them to roast the meat lining the shell.

Mayor León, in a pickup truck, brought word that Captain Conseco, the Federal man, would be here shortly.

"It's all right, he has the paper. But you'll have to sign it too before you can, ah, exhume the body."

Eric stood with his arms tightly crossed, staring at the crowd.

"It's great that they can find so much pleasure in a simple thing like drowning, isn't it?" he said to Polly.

A man set up a plank counter by the road, arranged large bottles of colored ice water on it, and sold drinks. Another, in an old army shirt and cotton pants, stood in the road fire-eating for the crowd.

Every time Eric looked around, someone was staring at him with a mournful look of sympathy. Then the person would sadly smile at him and nod.

About eleven, the cook stripped the flesh from the turtle shell and chopped it fine, then mixed it in the concave half of the shell with cooked rice, peppers, and onions. Another truck arrived with tubs of cracked ice and beer. Benches and a long table were set up for the guests of honor. Eric was introduced to these personages as they arrived—storekeepers, the druggist, two pretty sisters who were the town's teachers, a dozen others.

Finally a dusty jeep bearing Mexican army insignia rolled in and parked near the grave. The driver, a handsome man in a forest-green uniform and laced combat boots, brought a shovel and a paper to Eric. Over the crowd fell a hush like a fog.

"I am Captain Conseco," said the officer. "If you will sign here, you may proceed with the, ah, exhumation."

The captain had petulant, almost feminine, lips, a somewhat calculating face, pale eyes, and tousled hair. Eric had been thinking of refusing to go on with the farce, but the captain looked like someone who might jail a man for spoiling a party. He signed the paper; in exchange, the captain presented the shovel. A small black bow was tied to the handle of it.

Eric gazed around in panic. Polly smiled uncertainly and murmured something inaudible. Even she, Eric noticed, was somewhat overdressed, and had applied eye make-up. She had caught the fun-loving spirit of the exhumation.

Okay, you louses! he thought in bitterness. I hope whoever's in this grave haunts you forever.

As he advanced, people fell away before him as though he were a leper ringing a bell. He took hold of the cross and wrenched it from the ground. The thought registered dimly that it was exceptionally well painted, the enamel smooth and thick. The words, *El Gringo,* were actually carved into the wood.

As he began digging, tossing each shovelful onto the trail, the crowd closed in, silent and watchful. Sitting on the wall, Captain Conseco observed each flying shovelful of earth with a turn of his head like a judge at a tennis match.

The shovel struck wood.

Eric uttered a groan and looked up. In the front rank of watchers stood the old fisherman Lázaro, like a symbolic figure of death—Lazarus returned from the grave.

In an angry fever, Eric commenced pitching dirt right and left. Slowly the box came in view, seven feet long, three feet wide. The planks were splintered. One end was caved in. The top was broken, and down the center, like a keelson, ran a shredded two-by-three. It was the poorest excuse for a coffin he had ever seen.

Working the tip of the shovel beneath it, he tried to gauge the weight. It was so light that it rose several inches with the slightest leverage. A murmur rose from the crowd. A child cried and its mother shushed it. Eric knelt to examine the coffin. It was clear now that the box had only one end. Not only that, but there was a ring fixed in the bottom edge of one side. He sniffed. How cheap could you get? They had used a beaten-up old rowboat as a coffin!

He looked up, puzzled and resentful. Captain Conseco's mouth widened into a smile. Then he chuckled. Someone laughed. The crowd's mood broke. Everyone began to shriek and howl with laughter. The captain, helpless with shouts of falsetto laughter, came forward to grip Eric's shoulders.

"El Gringo was a boat, that's all—an old boat, *hombre!* Someone buried it and made a cross out of the transom. It was just a joke! But it *did* wash up on the beach!"

Big joke! Eric thought dazedly. Dumbly he stood there, angry and bewildered. Dr. Nestor came to him, chuckling.

"A little crude," he said. "I suppose they wanted to slow you down so that you wouldn't catch him. He made quite a hit. You'll just have to relax now and let them show you it was all in fun."

Eric decided to leave as soon as the banquet started.

chapter **23**

At the long table, two dozen guests lustily consumed the food Captain Gallardo's cook had prepared. Elsewhere among the trees, borderline guests sat on the ground to eat food they had brought. A fisherman carried the shieldlike turtle shell about the table as a tray and guests helped themselves to the food. The day had turned hot and muggy. Beer was going down in buckets; little bottles of water-clear tequila kept moving up and down the line.

A big man, purplish and toothless, swayed to his feet and tried to make a speech about brotherhood. Others shouted him down.

No one seemed to have noticed that Eric, after eating one plate of food, had not returned to the table. But at last Polly saw him packing his sea bag and hurried to him.

"Don't take it so hard!" she urged, holding his hands. "They were only having fun."

"I'm laughing, I'm laughing!" Eric said, yanking his hands away. He slapped a gnat crawling into his ear.

"It's just that they liked your father so much. And they like you too. They'll be hurt if you leave."

"Tough."

She watched him jam clothing into his sea bag. "Where are you going?"

"Ever hear of a place called Rancho Sereno? 'Where all your tomorrows are just like today.' That's what it says on the road signs. 'Today' may not have been much, but it was better than the tomorrows I've been having lately."

"It would be an international incident if you walked out on them!" Polly persisted.

Eric wadded all of Baja into one fist and shook it at her. "Sharks and mosquitoes and wind and sunburn . . . ! Baja should drop dead. El Rojo, too. He can get himself out of the nuthouse after they lock him up. I wash my hands of him."

He could see that Polly was laughing inside. She tried to take his hands, but he put them behind him.

"Don't do anything now," she begged. "Wait 'til tomorrow."

Someone was patiently standing nearby—the shark fisherman Lázaro, offering each a can of beer. The white hairs of his beard stood out like the quills of a porcupine. His expression was friendly. Under his arm he carried the gray paper parcel. It occurred to Eric that most of the oddballs he saw on the street carried parcels of some kind.

"*Una cerveza?*" said Lázaro.

"Thanks."

Polly, declining, continued to watch Eric with concern.

"No speaker Spanish?" Lázaro asked.

Eric nodded. "Speaker little. 'Stander much."

"Cómo?" said the old man.

Eric downed half the can of icy beer without breathing. He waited for a belch, then *"Sí, hablo español."*

Lázaro seemed happy and impressed. He switched to Spanish. "That's good. Most Americans can't say any more than, Hello, Good-bye, and Where is the beer?"

"I learned Spanish when I was a boy."

"Read English, too?"

Eric peered at him. *Was he kidding?* "Sure."

"Me, I don't read nothing. I fished with my father when I was very small. Cut bait, dressed sharks. Now I fish alone. Get sharks, pearls."

Eric glanced at Polly. I thought this guy was supposed to be antisocial, he thought. "Is that right?" he said. He imagined he could feel the beer buzzing in his head. Sniffing the food, he felt a solid jolt of hunger. "How about something to eat?" he said.

Lázaro wandered toward the table with him. "In the old days," he remarked, "they spoke differently."

"You mean, like 'thee' and 'thou'?"

Lázaro's head bobbed. "That's it!" he said, and, to Eric's surprise, gave a sly wink.

Man, this old boy is something else, Eric thought. "Art thou going to eat?" he asked.

Lázaro grinned. "Thank thee, no."

All the space was taken at the table, but room was made for Eric and Polly. Lázaro came over and stood behind Eric like a footman. Eric was embarrassed.

Across the table, Dr. Nestor was sweating profusely, a tortilla laden with food rolled in his hand. Polly said something to him that Eric could not hear, and he stared at Eric.

"Going back? Rubbish! You've got him cornered now, boy."

"Cornered like an eel," said Eric.

"It's only a few days more to La Paz. That's the capital. He's bound to be there, living it up."

"What if he isn't?"

"Then he'll be down at Cape San Lucas—that's the very tip of the peninsula. I guarandarntee you he won't turn the corner and sail back up the Pacific side. The open sea's too rough."

"As far as I'm concerned," Eric said flatly, "El Rojo could sink or swim and I wouldn't raise a hand."

He was looking for a tortilla when someone tapped his arm —Lázaro again. The old fellow leaned down to whisper in Eric's ear.

"You know where is the most beautiful place in the world? Isla Pichilingue, where I live! You should come out with me. I would show you how to kill a shark with a knife!"

"Thanks," Eric said, with a grimace. "If I ever get a chance, I'll take you up on it."

Nutty as a fruitcake, he thought.

There were speeches and toasts. Eric had to get up and say something about Mexican-American friendship. He suggested a highway for Baja. The guests cheered. Fernando said he was a good sport, and *muy macho,* like his father.

"Lock up your women," he told the others. "The redheads are coming! Maybe you'll catch him next time, *joven,*" he said happily to Eric. "Fifty pesos you drop the net over him in La Paz!"

The guests laughed, calling suggestions as to how to go about trapping a redheaded father.

"No, I've had it," Eric said.

"Had it? You mean you're going home?"

"That's what I mean," Eric said.

All the happy, perspiring faces immediately saddened. "He's going back!" the Mexicans said to each other. Word ran up and down the table. But instead of seeming happy that they had helped to turn back the menace, they appeared gloomy.

If I lived here the rest of my life, Eric thought, I'd never understand these cats.

Someone hushed the crowd while the two sisters who taught the children of the town rose to sing. Fernando strummed a few chords and they began singing, in whispers, a song called, "Silencio." In the midst of it, the purple-faced man stood up and started another speech. Someone pulled him down and gave him another beer.

At last the sun slanted in under the tops of the trees and people began to leave. Some who had been sleeping in the shade of the cemetery wall rose and shambled away. Everyone looked sweaty and stupefied. Captain Gallardo came to Eric, his eyes bloodshot.

"If you want to radio your mother," he said, "it will have to be soon. In an hour we leave. You can go out to the boat with me in the dinghy when I've seen to something in town."

"Thanks. I'll wait here, then," Eric said.

As he packed, Eric sank into a gravelike gloom. The hundreds of miles between here and San Felipe stretched away like a blue desert, to be excavated a paddleful at a time. Of course there was an easy way out: he could ask his mother to send a plane down for him. In fact she would probably insist on sending one, for it was her kind of scene—making him admit he had bitten off more than he could chew. And she was usually right.

Yes, but just think! a weasel voice in his mind piped. *By to-morrow night you could be home! Sleeping in a real bed! Pick-ing and singing with Flip and Henry! Calling up Joanie, slop-ping around the pool, riding the firebreaks on your motor-cycle . . . !*

No, no Ossa—another classic Eric boner. But everything else was just as it had been when he rode out; for nothing ever changed in Rancho Sereno. Tomorrow and today were synon-ymous; at least until your father flipped his lid.

"You're not leaving tonight, are you?" Polly, seated on the step of the camper, was watching him.

"No. Tomorrow."

"It's such a long way. Maybe you can get someone to go with you."

"What for? I got this far alone."

"Thanks," Polly said.

"No offense," said Eric.

"Dad says he'll loan you the money if you want to fly home."

"Forget it! I don't need anybody's help! If your dad had wanted to help, he could have told me what they were cooking up for me."

"My! What an awful mood you're in."

Conscious of a presence beside him, Eric glanced up. *Oh, no!* he groaned. *Not again.* It was Lázaro, offering the gray parcel he had carried around since yesterday!

"It's yours," said Lázaro.

Eric took the parcel from his hands, puzzled. The fisherman looked painfully earnest. Eric had begun to think of him as a rather clownish figure, but now again he saw the visage of the barehanded shark-killer, the hermit, the man not to be fooled with. He sensed that this was a pivotal moment.

"What is it?" he asked.

"See for yourself!"

Inside the package was a cone-shaped shell about five inches long, with a glassy surface. The brownish shell was intricately patterned with tiny triangular figures like sails. It lacked the class of a big queen conch, he thought, but was certainly unusual. He had never seen such a shell.

"*Muy bonito*," he said. "Thank you. Where did you find it?"

Lázaro shook his head, deadpan. Eric gathered that the question had been in poor taste. Polly came from the camper to look at the shell.

"I've never seen one like it. It's lovely. Dad!" she called. "Come and see this shell of Lázaro's."

"I'm resting," came a mournful voice from the camper.

"It's unusual. I think you should see it."

Puffy-eyed, the dentist came yawning from the camper, stuffing his shirttail in. " 'Drink not to elevation, nor eat to dullness,' " he muttered. "Let's see it."

He studied the shell. "Looks like a textile cone, but it's much finer." He asked Lázaro where he had found it. This time, Eric noticed, the old man's eyes narrowed with anger. He made no reply.

"I'll get my shell book," said Dr. Nestor. He returned with a fat green book and squatted down to turn pages, studying the shell. Suddenly he said:

"*Gloria maris!* But it's the wrong area."

"What's *Gloria maris?*"

"Glory-of-the-sea, a rare cone shell. The book says it's found primarily in the Philippines. According to this author, there are only about twenty specimens in existence. The old mossback!" he said. "I wish he'd tell us where he found it."

"Do you think I should take it?" Eric asked, dubiously. "It might be valuable."

"Certainly it's valuable. It says here specimens have sold for as much as twelve thousand dollars!"

Lázaro's mouth had tightened. He seemed to resent having his gift examined as though it might be somehow faulty. The situation, Eric recognized, was tricky. If you admired anything a Mexican owned, he would say, "It's yours." But if you accepted it, you had usually committed a gaffe. In this case the shell might well be worth more than everything Lázaro owned. Clearly, the thing to do was refuse it.

"I'd better give it back," he decided.

"It's hard to say," Dr. Nestor agreed. "He brought it as a gift. But it might easily bring a thousand dollars. And why should he give it to you? If he hasn't lost his mind, he must be up to something . . ."

Eric wrapped the shell and handed it to Lázaro. *"Mil gracias,"* he said. "But it's too fine, Lázaro. You could sell it."

The fisherman took the shell back. "As you wish," he said. He turned abruptly and walked from the camp.

Eric watched him go, not really surprised. "Don't miss the next episode of 'You Can't Win,'" he said wryly.

A few minutes later Captain Gallardo shouted, *"Apúrete! Let's go, joven!"* They went down to the river to his dinghy.

The radio connection was good. He heard his mother's voice distinctly; she said that she could hear him loud and clear. He told her he had missed his father again and was giving up. She was relieved. She tried to argue him out of coming back by canoe, but, seeming to realize that the gesture meant something to him, gave in.

"If that's really what you want to do . . ." she said.

Dully he gazed at the rust-pimples on the microphone. *Want to?* He didn't *want* to paddle anywhere. But he had to, so that people couldn't say, "Did you hear about Hansen? He paddled a canoe down to some hellhole in Baja, and his mother had to send a plane after him!"

The radioman took the mike and signed off. Eric insisted on paying him and Captain Gallardo a few dollars. Everyone seemed embarrassed, as though in giving up the chase he was doing something not exactly shameful, but not exactly prideful, either.

So close to catching El Rojo. But he was quitting! *Que lástima.*

As the dinghy carried him back, he sat unhappily examining a small coral cut on his right index finger. Little rays of infection fanned out from a tiny red crater. He squeezed a bit of pus from the wound and hoped it would not become serious.

Day broke hot and muggy. Eric lay on his sleeping bag sweating slightly as he listened to birds in the towering mango and papaya trees, to burros trotting by on the road and an occasional truck snorting and coughing as it passed.

Just below his wishbone was a caved-in area that would soon fill with anguish. This he knew from experience. He had fallen asleep thinking of his father, and awakened with thoughts of Polly. Sternly he reminded himself of the mean tricks she had played on him. But in the strong light of his feeling for her, these outrages faded like old photographs. He told himself that if he steered his emotions carefully, avoiding thinking of her, he would soon have forgotten the color of her eyes (dark green), and the feel of her fine, thick, silken hair in his hands. . . .

When he had dressed, there she was, slipping from the

camper in her bathrobe and making a finger-on-lips signal to him. He turned his back and started packing. He heard her come up, and out of the corner of his eye he saw her watching him.

"Eric, why don't you try it as far as La Paz?" she said.

"No use," he muttered.

She touched his arm. He kept packing. Polly crossed her arms and watched him. She stayed there while he finished rolling his sleeping bag and threw his belongings into the sea bag.

"Aren't you going to eat breakfast?" she asked.

"I'm not hungry," he said. Her long hair hung on her shoulders, and her eyes, still sleepy, looked sad.

"That's something new for you," she said, trying to joke.

Eric shouldered his gear and carried it to the boat. He was cheered to hear her following him. He stowed everything with care. At last he turned, and saw tears in her eyes.

"What's the matter?" he said.

She sniffled. "I'll probably never see you again."

"Is that so bad?" he said.

After a long, silent, hurt look, Polly turned to leave. Eric hesitated, then caught her arm. "I didn't mean it that way, Polly—I guess you know how I feel about you, but you've never said . . ."

In a moment, Polly, to his surprise, had turned back and was leaning against him: the only thing to do was to put his arms around her.

"How *do* you feel about me?" she whispered.

"If I told you that," said Eric, "you'd start bugging me again."

"No, I wouldn't," Polly promised, stirring slightly against him. He felt as though a pulse traversing him from head to heels had begun to beat like a drum.

"The way I feel," he said, "is this: if you were in the stands, I could cut ten minutes off my time for the two-mile."

Polly glanced up, smiled, looked carefully at his mouth, and turned her head slightly on the side before she kissed him. Eric closed his eyes; he opened them again, but, up so close, her face was a blur. He could tell only that her eyes were closed and her lashes were long. He drew a deep sigh, from the heels. Polly drew back and gazed at him with sleepy eyes that appeared very pale.

"I needed that!" Eric said.

Polly nuzzled his throat. "Don't go," she said.

He felt the tender trap closing on him. He sighed, reviewing all the arguments. Yet from here on, for hundreds of miles, he would be alone; and in the end El Rojo would be only a flash of red in the trees, that faded when you came too close.

"I've had it, Polly," he said. "When will you be back in San Francisco?"

"June," she said.

"I'll come up and see you after summer school."

"Bring some brochures on San Diego State," Polly said. "I'll go to work on Mother. I might go there next fall."

In a poignant mood, Eric paddled down the river and set sail north. When he was not thinking about Polly, he thought about his father. But trailing him was pointless—the bloodhound sniffing along a stone-cold trail.

With the wind almost in his teeth, he made poor mileage that day. At dusk he made camp on a beach in view of Isla Pichilingue, Lázaro's hideout. Its flat bulk seemed to sink into the blood-red water like a swimming crocodile. Night fell and Eric made his fire and cooked some food. Afterward, he lay on his elbow gazing at the sea where the island had been absorbed into the darkness. He wondered where the fisherman had his camp, and whether he could see his campfire at this distance. He was sorry he had refused the old man's shell.

Hearing footsteps in the coarse sand, he twisted to gaze behind him. It was like a supernatural occurrence to see Lázaro standing there, his spiky white beard and hair tinted by the firelight. In his hands Lázaro held an antique rifle with a bore big enough to fire tennis balls.

Lázaro said, "Put your things in your boat. We will have to go to the island tonight so that no one will see us together. Otherwise they might send someone to search for you some day."

chapter **24**

Several times during the night Eric woke to see Lázaro sitting cross-legged on the sand near him, smoking a bitter-smelling Mexican cigarette. The rifle lay across his lap. They had come in the two boats in an hour and ten minutes—he had timed it—and made camp on a beach in a tiny cove. Lázaro had had him place rocks in his canoe and sink it in several feet of water. Now, as far as the outside world could tell, Eric Hansen had never set foot on Isla Pichilingue. He had simply vanished.

The last time he opened his eyes it was dawn. He peered around. The cove was so small that it looked like a model for a full-sized cove to be constructed later. The two rocky horns guarding its entrance curved to within a couple of hundred yards of each other. Dark cliffs fell straight to the water. But where the beach was, at the apex of the cove, the cliffs were less precipitous, with evidence of benches above.

He heard goats bleating. Sitting up, he saw a little herd of a dozen animals crossing the sand toward them, a brown and white dog herding them. Lázaro said warningly to Eric, "*Cuidado!*" He greeted the dog as it came frisking up, then rummaged in his boat, the rifle in the crook of his arm, and found a plastic bucket. Two of the goats were nannies; he knelt to milk them. The dog poked around near Eric, barking at him now and then.

Eric had not accepted the proposition that he was in danger of being murdered. But he was obviously in deep trouble. A memory came of a story he had read. A man was held captive in the jungle by another man who liked Dickens. The captor could not read. So the prisoner spent the rest of his life reading Dickens to him.

All the talk Friday about whether he could read and write —did that mean anything? Was he to spend the rest of his life reading *Don Quixote* aloud?

Lázaro rose with a half-pail of goat's milk. "Let's go!" he said.

"Is this Pichilingue?" Eric asked.

"Yes. I live in a cave up there. Bring all you can carry."

"What's the idea?" asked Eric.

"You and your arrogant manners," said Lázaro.

Eric said earnestly, "I'm sorry about the shell! But it was too fine to accept."

"I tried to be your friend. Since you didn't care for my friendship, we will try it as enemies."

"But—"

"Hurry up!"

Eric walked toward a trail Lázaro pointed out at the base of a cliff. The trail was well graded. After climbing a short time, he looked down and noticed something: holes were dug in the cliff at a number of points, as though someone had been prospecting. Judging by the piles of rock, some were thirty or forty feet deep.

In ten minutes they reached a bench. Here was a stone corral for the goats, a line for drying meat; tools and several trees, a stone-and-cement water tank about the size of a wading pool; a small stone cookshack, and the rocked-up entrance of a cave. Above the entrance to the cave hung an enormous set of shark jaws. Near the cliff was a small pyramid of rocks into which was set a picture postcard of the Virgin of Guadalupe. Candle stubs adorned it.

"Sit there," said Lázaro, pointing.

Eric sat in a hide chair while the fisherman penned his goats. Lázaro poured milk into two pottery cups and set the balance inside the cave. He handed Eric one of the cups. The goat's milk was warm and revolting. He gagged.

Lázaro made coffee and set a bag of *pan dulce* on a crude table. Eating, Eric studied the cove below. The water graded from clear green to blue-black. A large yacht could anchor in this cove. No doubt some had tried; but Lázaro would know how to scare them off.

The old man brushed crumbs from his white whiskers. Did he trim them, Eric wondered, or did they break off like quills when they were an inch long?

"All right," said Lázaro. "Now I will show you why you are here. I would have made you a partner. But since you had to be so high and mighty you are now merely working for me."

From the cove he brought something wrapped in paper. He squatted and unwrapped a piece of sheet copper about the size of a page from a book. Nail holes punctured one edge. One side of it was green with corrosion; the other side was polished.

"Well, you with your learning, what does it say?" Lázaro sneered.

Eric studied the rough printing scratched into the copper. The crude characters resembled cuneiform writing. The first word appeared to be STAN, followed by a triangle. The triangle might be a D. STAND.

Lázaro snatched the copper from his hand. "Read it to me, not to yourself!" he shouted.

Eric flinched. "It's hard to read! I *think* it's English, but the letters are peculiar."

Lázaro reached out to lay his hand on the stock of his rifle. "And don't think you can make up something and go away, because you will stay in any case until we find it."

"Find what?"

From his pocket, Lázaro took a coin. It was as large as a dollar, but it was gold.

"The rest of the treasure," he said.

Eric inspected the gold coin Lázaro handed him. The words on it were in Latin. There was a bust of a ruler on one side, a coat of arms on the other. The coin had surprising weight and a slippery feel. He handed it back.

"Is that why you dug all the holes?" he asked.

"I've dug for eight years; and I'll dig another eight if I have to."

"Alone?"

"Sure, alone. I work my guts out. But now I've got a helper." He bared his teeth like a dog trying to smile.

"My parents will send boats and planes to find me," Eric said, his mouth suddenly dry.

"Not after your canoe washes up on some beach. If we don't find the gold right away, I'll set your boat adrift upside down. They'll figure you drowned."

Eric's heart shriveled in terror. Lázaro was withholding the rest of the story. He was too sly ever to let him go, knowing Captain Conseco would come immediately with a boatload of Federal police. He was not saying that, the day the treasure was found, he would kill his captive.

His voice reedy, Eric asked, "Why don't you dig where you found this coin?"

"I have, years ago. Do you think I'm crazy? Later I found the copper plate. It was under a foot of silt in my own cave, by God! Here is where they camped, the pirates. One of them called Cromwell hung around La Paz Bay. Now take this again and read it to me!"

Seven lines of characters had been scratched into the metal. The *S* in STAND consisted of three straight lines, *slant left, slant right, slant left.*

The second word started with another triangle; this one was bisected horizontally. It could be a B. The second character was an arrow pointing left. The third was clearly an H, and after that came I, N, and another triangle. Suddenly he saw that the arrow had to be an E: BEHIND.

" *'Stand behind . . .'* " he read aloud, in Spanish.

Lázaro made a choking sound. Eric looked at him. There were tears in his eyes. The old man lowered his head to hide them. He raised his face after a moment.

"Is it English for sure?" he said.

"I think so. But some of the letters are different. . . ." Eric wiped his hand over the copper, as though removing the obscurities. Haltingly he read:

STAND BEHIND BLACK
BOVLDER   BRING
TAP IN LINE WITH
HILL AN RIGHT
SOVTH IAA FATHAMS
IT LIES IN TWA FATHAMS
NEAR BLACK CLIFF

"That's it," he said.

Lázaro scrambled up and gazed out over the cove. "*All* the cliffs are black!" he groaned.

"What about the black boulder?"

"These rocks crumble. In two hundred years, what would be left?"

Eric pointed. "There's a flat boulder there, near the water —the one with the pelican sitting on it."

"Yes! It must have been very big at one time. You're right."

The hill on the right.

Far out on the right-hand horn of the cove was a pyramidal peak. Eric pointed it out.

"*Eso!*" Lázaro turned quickly. "Where are your diving things?"

"On the beach."

Lázaro hurried to the shrine, knelt and said a prayer. Eric caught the word, *tiburones.* Sharks.

When they left, the old man still carried the gun, but was less vigilant about keeping Eric covered. They stood behind the black boulder to take a sighting on the peak. The cove opened to the south. The peak rose on the west side of the inlet. A black cliff overhung the water, almost directly in line with the hill.

"That's it!" Lázaro said.

chapter **25**

One hundred fathoms equaled two hundred yards. Having run the two-twenty, Eric was able to estimate the distance. With deep strokes of the paddle, Lázaro moved the *panga* across the water. The boat skimmed the sandy beach, then passed a shore littered with rocky debris; now the cliffs loomed on their right. Eric had picked as his point of reference a *cardón* cactus leaning outward from the black cliff.

When they reached it, Lázaro told him to lower the anchor. There were fathom knots in the rope and Eric counted them as the anchor went down. Four knots—twenty-four feet.

"Four fathoms," Lázaro said. "Too deep, but we'll start here and work in. About the sharks. It is not true that I hate them, nor that I love them, as you may have heard. I keep an eye on them. I fish for sharks outside the cove; that's where they belong. Here they are not welcome. Take this knife . . ."

He pushed a sheathed knife toward him with his sandal. Eric was almost afraid to pick it up. Was he trying, in his mind, to justify killing him? *"I didn't like the way he grabbed that knife, so I killed him. . . ."*

Finally he reached down and picked it up. Lázaro watched keenly.

"Be careful," he said. "I use a knife better than you. The sharks, now. Big ones seldom forage inside the cove. If you see one, come up at once. The little ones are curious and sometimes get too close. Bang them on the nose with a rock or the handle of your knife. If one refuses to leave and you have to kill him, it's done like this—" "Drive your knife into the body just behind the pectoral fins," he said, "and rip back. Disembowel him, then rush for the boat."

Eric nodded. He would swim for the boat the first time he saw a shark of any size. Fight sharks yourself, shark man.

"What are we looking for?" he asked.

"For anything strange—rusty metal—weed growing in the shape of a boat."

The diving filled the morning. Curious fish congregated. Twice Eric had to rest and warm himself. Once Lázaro sat in the boat smoking a cigarette with meager puffs, his diving goggles hanging about his neck. He wore old white shorts with rusty stains. They ate stale rolls and slices of papaya for lunch, then dived again. The sun set. Eric was bone-weary.

Paddling back, Lázaro looked as fresh as ever. Dr. Nestor should take blood samples from him, thought Eric—he is definitely a rough-water animal.

In the evening, Lázaro fried a fish he had speared. He heated refried beans. The *chiverro* drove the goats into the corral and Lázaro fed him.

Eric slept on a cot the old man carried from the cave. Twice that night he opened his eyes to see the old man lying on his side gazing out over the water. Did he never sleep?

The next day Lázaro made driftwood stakes and carried them and some old fishing line to the diving site. On the bottom, he drove the stakes into wedges in the rocks, then stretched lines between them to mark out areas to be searched. Thus there was no duplication of effort, nor any area left unsearched.

At four o'clock on the third day, Eric found a piece of corroded brass near the cliff. He swam with it to the boat. Lázaro was sharpening a stake with his knife. He took the piece of green metal and examined it. With his knife he scraped off the corrosion and encrusted shells.

"An oarlock!" he exclaimed. "A broken oarlock!"

"It could have come from any boat," Eric told him.

"They haven't made oarlocks like this for a hundred years!"

They swam down together. As they were scrutinizing the place where Eric had found it, a shadow crossed above their heads. Lázaro glanced up. Eric saw the white belly of a large fish disappearing into the bluish gloom of deep water. Gesturing, Lázaro told him to return to the boat. Before he could do so, however, the shark came rushing back. It was a large fish with a half-moon mouth. It began circling them slowly.

Paralyzed, Eric crouched on the bottom. The shark appeared to be ten or twelve feet long, not the size you intimidated.

Suddenly Lázaro swam directly at the shark, knife glinting

in the greenish light. The shark veered aside. Lázaro went in like a tiger, drove the knife to the hilt in the shark's abdomen, ripped it back. Blood exploded in the water like smoke from a grenade. Eric shoved off, burst into the sunlight, reached the boat, and crawled in. Lázaro came right behind him, breathing hard. Water dripped from his whiskers. He looked like some sort of sea creature, a mutation of a sea lion.

"Brute!" he said.

"L-l-let's go!" Eric chattered.

"No, no. I'll go down and bring him up after while. The oil in his liver will keep; and did you see his fins? Lots of soup in those fins."

"Okay, but no more diving for me today," Eric said firmly.

Lázaro glanced up at the sky. "You're right, it's getting late."

This old aborigine is too much, Eric thought.

Eric awoke weary enough to sleep another ten hours. But by full light they were diving. Lázaro stretched new lines and dug in the coarse sand with a bar. Eric seemed to spend most of his time hanging onto the boat, recharging his lungs like tired batteries.

Suddenly, excited, Lázaro came up to clutch Eric's arm.

"Come and look at this!"

They swam down. What he had found under a foot of cobbles was a layer of gravel. Pallid ghost-shrimp scurried about. He had cleared an area about two feet square. Down the middle of it ran a stripe of darker gravel. They surfaced.

"Did you see it?" he panted.

"Yes. What is it?"

"A piece of wood once lay there. When it rotted, it stained the gravel! Maybe it was the gunwale of a boat. . . ."

They cleared more of the bottom to the depth of the gravel; the stain continued in a straight line. But now it passed under a boulder as large as a safe. Lázaro attacked it with a crowbar: the boulder stood fast. He surfaced, breathed deeply for several minutes to oxygenate his bloodstream, then submerged.

Floating face-down, Eric watched him drive the bar under the rock at a new angle, then set himself like Atlas and lift. For a full half-minute he held the position, straining every muscle. Through his faceplate Eric saw the agony deepen in his face. The boulder gave up first; slowly it canted to one side.

By nightfall, the stone had been moved away. Lázaro clawed at the gravel and found that the stain continued. Before the light grew too dim, they traced the discoloration string-straight another six feet before it passed under another large rock.

The next day Eric found a long greenish stain that Lázaro said was copper. Then they found a second brown stain eight feet to the right of the first and paralleling it.

"The other side of the boat!" Lázaro announced.

He worked faster, tumbling rocks about, clawing at the gravel, stretching strings. Eric felt now that the fisherman was right: it had been a boat. Whatever the map was meant to locate, the boat was involved in the mystery. Perhaps the treasure had been placed in a longboat and the boat sunk. Later, when some danger passed, it could have been raised.

Just before nightfall, Lázaro burst from the water to yell:

"The lines come together!"

Eric swam down to look. It was true: the two stains converged in a sharp V like the prow of a boat!

Paddling to the beach, Lázaro could not contain his excitement. "That's it! We've done it. All that remains is to excavate it!" Playfully, he splashed water with the paddle onto Eric.

Eric grinned, sure now that Lázaro's mind had crossed a Great Divide. "Now you don't need me any more," he suggested.

"But I do! A boat like that might be five feet deep. Much work ahead! Besides, you can't leave until I've found the treasure, so that I can hide it before you tell Captain Conseco about me. If I let you go now, it would still be on the bottom when they come."

He paddled with crazy speed, his face cracking into laughter lines, scars of exhaustion, white teeth. Eric crashed to the floor as the boat jarred on the beach. Lázaro laughed.

"*Cuidado, joven!* You don't learn anything!"

From the rocks came the bleating of goats and the yelping of the *chiverro*. Lázaro leaped out and rushed across the sand to greet the dog. He picked him up in his arms and danced around.

"Juanito, you are a rich dog! I will buy you canned food and you can retire!"

Eric sat on the thwart, watching. A blade of fear and joy drove into his heart. He was alone in the boat; Lázaro was a hundred feet away sporting with the dog. How fast could Lázaro swim? Not as fast as a canoe going full blast, nor for very far. He gave a shiver.

Lázaro set the dog on the sand and began chasing the goats toward the cliff trail, yelling and hooting at them. Eric put a shaking hand on the paddle lying at his feet. He picked it up. Then, his eyes on the fisherman, he thrust it over the side and began pushing the boat out. The keel grated in sand; whispered; slipped free.

Eric faced forward. He gave another couple of pushes with the paddle, then began with desperate force and quietness to stroke. . . .

A scream tore the evening, a curse. Eric slashed at the water and the *panga* began to move, sluggish as a passenger liner leaving the pier. Eric looked back. He had hardly left shore and Lázaro was halfway across the sand.

Digging furiously at the water, he kept his eyes on the narrow aperture a half-mile ahead. He heard Lázaro splash into the water. Bending forward, he stroked savagely, tearing the water into foam. The canoe began to swing to the left; he took a stroke on the left side and corrected its course. With each stroke he dipped the paddle so hard that he lifted himself off the thwart.

Behind him the sound of swimming was closer. He threw a glance back. Lázaro was swimming much faster than the canoe was moving. In his teeth he carried a knife. Eric moaned. The paddle struck the side of the boat and was twisted out of his grasp. It fell overside and floated behind. He sobbed, flung himself forward to get the other paddle, but before he could secure it, a dripping hand seized the stern of the canoe. Lázaro's crazy face appeared, knife and teeth glinting, beard dripping.

Eric dived into the water. Without knowing for sure what he was doing, he knew where he was going: to the hillside south of camp. He would go over the ridge to the west side of the island. He would hide out tonight, signal someone in the morning.

He looked back once. He was gaining. He had the knife at his belt, nothing else. No shoes, matches, food. He reached the shallows, but it was rocky, impossible to wade ashore speedily. Meanwhile the fisherman closed the gap between them. Soon he, too, was wading. Eric stumbled from the water. The red volcanic rocks, porous as sponge, but sharp, cut his feet. He limped, staggered, headed up the hill. After a short time he blundered into a narrow path like an animal trail. Stumbling, he followed it. The trail slanted upward toward the ridge.

He saw something that caused him to hesitate. Beside the trail stood a cross. Gasping, he looked at it. The cross told its own story: Lázaro had not mentioned having a wife or partner. But someone was buried here. So he must have had another helper at one time. . . .

Eric started running again. Behind him he heard Lázaro racing. A rock snagged his toe; he gasped with pain and fell. He heard Lázaro behind him. He fumbled for his knife, but he was too late.

The fisherman stood above him.

chapter **26**

Lázaro stood gasping for breath, too winded to speak. Eric stared up at him, sick with terror: his bowels, his brain, his heart, had turned to jelly. He lay there waiting for the pain.

Lázaro, panting, said, "Blockhead! What was the idea?"

Eric did not reply.

"You saw the cross?" Lázaro gasped.

Dumbly, Eric waited.

"I buried him! I didn't leave him for the buzzards, did I?" Lázaro was arguing with himself. "God won't hold it against me. I burn candles for his soul, too."

Eric saw a crack of light in the dungeon. "God holds murder against you," he said. "Forever."

"It wasn't murder! How do *you* know? You weren't here. It was five years ago."

"You'd go to Purgatory!" Eric said.

Lázaro made a slashing gesture with the knife, his face distorting. 'Go to Purgatory yourself! He tried to kill me."

"*I* didn't try to kill you," Eric said.

"That's different. He followed me all the way from Mazatlán! Beached his boat across the island and sneaked up on me. He had a pistol. He shot at me and I played dead. But when he got close, I jumped up and used my knife. It was him or me."

"Who was he?" Eric asked.

"Some pimp of a bank clerk! I had found four of the gold coins, and I had to have money. I knew what would happen if I tried to use them in Bahía Escondida. A gold rush! So I sailed across the Gulf, hundreds of miles south, and went into a bank. I told him, 'Here's a gold piece for you, if you will be quiet.' He gave me money, and then what? He followed me here and tried to kill me."

Lázaro sheathed the knife and stepped away. There were tears in his eyes, grief and anger in his face.

"Why did you have to spoil it? I felt so good. Damn you!"

"Because I don't want to die. And you'll kill me when you've got the treasure. So *I* don't feel good."

Lázaro struck his chest. "Am I a murderer?" he shouted. "I *told* you I'd let you go. I wanted to be your friend. God knows I'm a lonesome man. Goats and a dog—I'm crazy with lonesomeness! But how can a treasure hunter have friends?"

Eric told him, "If you let me go, I wouldn't tell anybody. But I don't suppose you'd believe that."

"I don't care whether you tell or not! I'll hide the money

where nobody will find it. And it's your word against mine about kidnaping you. So if you're unharmed what can they do to me?"

Eric picked up a small stone and rubbed it. "Sure. That's right." In surprise, he realized that it probably was right. Lázaro did not need to kill him. It was one man's word against another's.

"Sure it is." Lázaro put the knife away. "Well, let's beach the boat and have dinner. Do you like wine? I've got some I save for special times. Do you know how many special times I have? I've had the wine for two years without opening it. Isn't that a laugh?"

They set off. Going down the trail beside Eric, he suddenly put his arm across his shoulders.

"Two years and nothing to celebrate! Not since I found a pearl worth fifty dollars."

A gut-deep note sounded in Eric's being. It vibrated in his bones. He felt lightheaded and happy. For the unbelievable thing was not only that suddenly he felt sorry for the old man but that, in some way, he felt brotherhood for him.

They cleared the area outlined by the stains of rotten wood and corroded copper fittings. Starting at the bow, they worked back, excavating stones, sand, and shells from the hull. On a narrow ledge at the water line they piled the artifacts as they found them. A bronze anchor. Some brass spoons, lead musket balls, bottles, a silver crucifix. But no treasure chest, and as they neared the stern of the longboat they began to work more slowly, afraid to finish and realize failure.

Then one morning Eric felt his shovel grate oddly when he sank it in the sand. He raked his fingers through the area and felt something smooth. He pulled up a flat, irregular object like the five-ring symbol of the Olympic games—a cluster of silver coins corroded together! A single gold coin fell from the cluster.

When he surfaced, yelling, Lázaro was in the boat warming himself. Eric shouted and held the coins aloft. He swam to the canoe. Lázaro took the coins. Eric started chattering, but the old man was not listening. He gazed at the coins with his head lowered; his eyes were closed, and he was praying in Spanish.

Eric adjusted his face mask to submerge again, but Lázaro put his hand on his shoulder. "No more," he said softly.

"We've got it now!" Eric yelled. "It's the chest they sank the treasure in! Come on . . . !"

Lázaro smiled. "Perhaps. But two men with much gold is like two men with one woman. It's asking for trouble. I'll finish it myself. Tomorrow you must go."

He took Eric to the beach, then returned to dive some more, alone. When he returned later to the cave where Eric was eating lunch, a soft light was in his face.

Lázaro collected food for Eric's trip; they had eaten most of what he had brought. He assembled dried goat's meat, canned beans, a couple of papayas, plenty of stale rolls. They removed the rocks from Eric's boat and raised it; drying on the beach, it looked better and tighter than ever.

In midafternoon Lázaro started barbecuing a kid he had butchered a couple of days before. He made a spicy sauce and basted the meat over a fire in a small pit. As evening fell, the fragrance of smoke and roasting meat stirred an old, stone-age magic in Eric's heart. He sighed, and drowsed with a smile on his face, drowning in content.

The goat meat, tender and sweet, fell off the bones as they devoured it. Greedily they stripped the ribs. Eric sat back to contemplate the cove, dark now and with a path of hammered moon-gold across it.

"I wish I had met your father," Lázaro said. "The people liked him."

Groggy and happy, Eric said, "He must have gotten *muy simpatico* after he came down here. He was plenty jumpy when he left."

"What was wrong with him? Was he afraid of something?"

Eric grinned at the fisherman.

"He's got the same problem you've got now, Lázaro: nothing to do! When you get that gold to the bank, you'll be just like him."

Lázaro raised his hands. "Me? I've got plenty to do! When I get my money, I'm going to buy a motorboat and dive for black pearls! This peninsula was famous for them once. Then the pearl oysters died out. But I know where there's a fine bed that's never been touched, and when I get my money I'll harvest the pearls before the pearl-vultures know what I'm up to. Don't worry about me. I've got secrets that would keep a man busy for two lifetimes."

Eric smiled drowsily and pondered it. Maybe Lázaro did, maybe he didn't. He'd called the shot on this one, but he'd probably used up his luck for a while. At any rate, he would keep busy.

"The trouble with my father," he said, "was that he didn't know he had a problem until it was too late. He was just sitting there going into dry rot. And I guess I was getting the same problem from watching him, because I didn't know what I wanted to do either."

"But now you know?"

Eric blinked. "Well, no. Not exactly . . . but I'll know it when I see it. The thing to do is to go in full bore—tear a thing apart and see what's ticking inside. Try it on. That's what I've been thinking lately. Like Dr. Nestor. Maybe I'll be a marine biologist. I think I'd like that. And he has another problem—my dad, I mean. I don't know what he can do about it, though. I didn't realize it was a problem before. But it is."

"His woman?" asked Lázaro.

Eric hesitated. "Uh, yeah—my mother. She kind of runs things, I think."

"The women should run some things," Lázaro said. "But not all. I see American women once in a while. They wear pants and shout like boys. Are they men or women? They don't seem to know, and the men don't know enough to tell them to shut up."

"That's it," Eric said, nodding. "That's it right there. This girl I brought down with me—she's a very nice girl. But she began to think she should run the show. That's where I had to straighten her out. And after I got her straightened out she seemed happier."

Lázaro nodded wisely. "Sure! Everybody's happier."

In the morning, the sun woke Eric. Sea birds dived and swooped above the island. A pelican was fishing the cove; high above, suspended in the pure rosy quartz of the sky, a black frigate bird drifted south as steadily as a satellite. Eric heard Lázaro humming to himself as he worked at the stove. The old man, he saw, was filled with contentment such as most men never even got a taste of. They didn't, because you had to eat a lot of hard luck before you could savor the taste of victory. Eight years of digging holes, diving, and fighting sharks! He'd earned his joy. Gold was not the only reason for his joy, but the satisfaction of completing the struggle he had started when he found the coin and the map.

He compared his own struggle—paddling a canoe for a

couple of weeks before giving up. He had been like a home-sick child leaving summer camp early. He must have looked ridiculous to the Mexicans, whose lives were a mosaic of struggle.

Sitting up, he shook out his tennis shoes, mindful of scorpions. Something fell out of one of them—the glory-of-the-sea shell. Inside the shell Lázaro had wedged the gold coin.

Eric finished dressing. He stood before the cookshack with his hands in his pockets. When Lázaro emerged with the smudged blue coffeepot, he said,

"Many thanks, old-timer."

"It's nothing," said Lázaro.

Afterward, they carried his things down to the beach and loaded the canoe. Facing each other on the sand, they gripped hands.

"Good luck, boy," said Lázaro.

"Luck to you, too."

Lázaro gave him the *abrazo*. "Don't spend the coin for a while," he said. "I'll need time to finish here."

"I'll never spend it," Eric said. "Good-bye!"

He paddled from the cove. In the breeze outside, he set a course for the west side of the island. Once there, he turned for a last look at Pichilingue. A pelican crashed into the water near him He adjusted the jib, sat in the bottom of the boat with his hand on the tiller, and headed south, to finish what he had started when he left Rancho Sereno on his motorcycle.

chapter 27

El Rojo was not at Isla Carmen, though he had indeed been there. He had visited other places along the coast also, but only his memory had lingered, in the minds of a fishing family or two, a lighthousekeeper, the master of a fishing boat. Somewhere he had acquired a supply of twenty-two-caliber rifle shells, and he had left a box or two at each little coastal ranch home where he was fed or passed a night. They were of inestimable value to families who valued a rabbit as food or detested him as a spoiler of cornfields. He was, evidently, at last out of pliers.

One night Eric beached his boat near the cactus-branch shelter of two *vagabundos*. They were clannish, meeting with coldness his attempts to make conversation. He built his fire some distance away, put food to cook, then set to work reinforcing, with needle and thread, the clew of his mainsail. The men watched, interested. He was bungling the job, and knew it, but muttering under his breath he kept stitching, for the brass ring was working out and soon the sail would tear.

Presently the *vagabundos* drifted over. They were lean, unshaven men with dull black hair and the bodies of underfed tigers.

"No, no, *hombre,*" one of them said. "Not with that kind of thread."

In his hand he carried a spool of waxed linen. He sat on the sand beside Eric and showed him the stitch. Eric took the needle and a leather pad to push it with, and started over. The fishermen watched closely.

"That's it! . . . No, take two stitches there. Now you've got it."

Afterward they pooled their dinner. Eric told them about the close call with the sharks.

"There's an old man on Isla Pichilingue who kills sharks barehanded!" one of the men said. "With a knife, and plenty of heart. He's crazy, of course."

"Is that a fact?" Eric said. "With a knife, eh?"

They told him about it. They had Lázaro gouging the shark's eyes out, then tormenting him savagely. He lived entirely on shark meat, and was said to have a faint odor of shark flesh! It was known that the old man had killed and buried a number of wayfarers on his island.

"If you see him coming, paddle like the devil!"

One day he made a smoky landfall west of a very large island. A few smaller islands broke the slaty surface of an

enormous bay. From the quantity of smoke above the peninsula, he knew that he was approaching La Paz, the capital of
Baja California Sur. Soon he was in a scattered traffic of small
ships and swordfish boats plying the bay. Miles of palm trees
lined a long waterfront. Behind them, a drab expanse of buildings reached back to tawny desert hills. He could see that it
was quite a city, wide and low, the color of the earth from
which it had been built.

"*If he isn't there, he'll be at Cape San Lucas, the tip of the
peninsula.*"

Dr. Nestor had told him that. The cape was another three
or four days by canoe, though only a few hours by road; and
while the thought of missing him in La Paz was depressing, it
did not crush him as had his early failures. Failure was something you could get used to, he realized. He had become a
journeyman loser. Losing skillfully, he sensed, was a much
more important art than was winning, since you did more of
it.

He sailed past a pier where rusty little freighters were tied
up and freight was being borne down gangplanks by small,
muscular men wearing greasy headbands. Beyond the pier lay
the heart of the city, a congregation of old and new buildings,
and clots of greenery. Drifting, he dreamed of a hotel room
and a hot shower: there were miles of beachfront to search,
and he did not feel like searching. Besides, this was not the
sort of beach one camped on. The water was green and murky
and sewage tainted the air. He might find the yellow *panga*,
but the *vagabundo* would be living it up in some clean hotel.

He beached his boat near a low sea wall barring the sand
from a palm-lined street. Standing on the wall, he studied the
scene. A customs office stood across the street, a large old
hotel to the left. Blank-walled structures ran off to the right.

A highly polished Chevrolet of a vintage year paused before him and the driver peered out at Eric.

"Taxi?"

He got in front. A shrine with a red light in it was fixed to the dashboard; pictures of baseball players were pasted beside it. There was infinite luxury in the padded seat. Eric squirmed about on it.

"Is there a hotel that will take a *vagabundo?*" he asked.

The driver laughed. "You look like one, boy! There's a place outside town that might take you. The manager's a good judge of character. That's what you're going to need."

He parked before a small hotel in the suburbs. Date palms and big-leaved plants made the forecourt cool and green. A fattish young man in sunglasses was washing down an enormous bougainvillaea that cascaded from the roof. The driver got out and talked to the man, who turned off the water. The man in the sunglasses looked Eric over as he stood beside the taxi.

"I'll have to talk to the boss," he said.

In a few minutes a very small, neat man emerged. He shook hands with Eric while his eyes appraised him keenly.

"I have only one room left," he said. "You mean to shave and clean up, eh? I have only American guests, who aren't accustomed to natives."

"Show me a shower!" Eric said.

"No women or rough stuff? No drunkenness?" said the manager.

"No, no. Actually, I'm looking for my father . . ."

The man peered at him, then called excitedly to the man in the sunglasses. "Look at this boy, Arturo! Does he remind you of anyone?"

"Mr. Hansen! The living image!"

"He was here last week," the manager told Eric. "He stayed five days with us."

"Where did he go?"

"To Todos Santos, on the Pacific side. You can get a taxi driver to take you there."

"Twenty-five dollars," the taxi driver said promptly. "All-day trip."

Eric was too tired to bargain. "I'll talk to you in the morning," he said.

The lobby was empty. So was a tile-floored lounge beyond, where a Siamese cat slept on a couch eight feet long. The manager led Eric to a room off a tropical garden. The room was large and airy and had the hushed coolness of a chapel. He showered and shaved; then, feeling clean and relaxed, he drowsed on the bed thinking of Polly.

In the morning he arranged with the taxi driver to be taken to Todos Santos. It was about a three-hour drive, the man said. Mr. Hansen's son, eh? How about that? Arturo was telling me. Your father got my friend Alfredo's windshield wipers working again. It was a little hole in the vacuum line from the carburetor! He spotted it right off.

For most of the morning, as it crossed the peninsula, the taxi raced along a graded road through dry jungles of barbed desert growth. At last it whined up over a stony ridge, and Eric instantly felt the blessing of sea air, like cool hands on his face. The road dropped steeply; they were looking down into a vision of greenery—treetops, canefields, lofty mango groves, and an intricate network of canals. A couple of miles west sparkled the Pacific. The driver explained that a river burst from the hillside nearby, no one understood how, and created this jewel of tropical growth.

As they rolled toward the town, people beside the road held

up jars of water like symbolic offerings. "What's in the jars?" Eric asked.

"Little fish! An American tried to raise tropical fish here last year. But he was a boozer, and didn't tend to business. His tanks overflowed and now the ditches are full of little red and black fish. The people catch them with tea strainers and sell them."

The streets of the town climbed and descended, meandering without plan. The taxi crossed canals by small stone bridges. Finally they reached a small, dusty plaza. Ranged about it were small stores and *cantinas,* a two-storied wooden hotel, and a big Chinese general store.

The driver said, "He'd probably be staying in the hotel, if he's in town. We'll ask at the hotel *cantina,* where everything is known."

Now that he was so close, Eric felt hypnotized, practically nailed to the seat. By an almost physical effort, he roused himself to follow the driver into the *cantina.* Three Mexicans sat at a table; two others leaned on the bar, observing him. The bartender sat on a high stool delicately plucking at a guitar on his lap. He was bald, and had a plump brown nose like one of the little bananas called *dominicos.*

"Oiga, Felipe," said the driver. "This young man is looking for his father. His name is Hansen, and—"

"Mr. Hansen?" said the barman brashly. "Glad to meet you, Mr. Hansen. Mr. Hansen, your father, is out at his plantation, Mr. Hansen."

Eric sat on a stool. His plantation, eh? But he was beyond surprise, and looked at the bartender calmly. "His plantation?"

Felipe laid the guitar aside and stood up. "He's leased the tropical fish farm," he said to the driver.

"Ah," said Eric. "When was this?"

"Last week. And of course all the trees on it. But what he seems to be interested in is the fish. He is rebuilding the tanks and constructing fountains. We are happy to see it restored. There will be jobs."

"Where is it?"

"I know where it is," said the driver impatiently. "We passed it coming in. Let's go."

They piled back into the cab. In five minutes they swung into a grove of mango trees and crossed a canal. Beyond the canal were acres of farmland threaded by ditches. In odd patterns among the ditches were shallow, rectangular ponds lined with black sheet plastic. Some of the tanks were half-full of algae and water lilies. Others were empty. Lengths of dusty hose lay about like dead snakes. On a hilltop Eric saw a large, low house.

The driver pointed at a man standing near one of the ponds. "Is that your father?"

Eric squinted. A tall, red-haired man was mixing cement in a flat box. He wore dungarees and a dirty tee shirt, and had a stubble of reddish beard. Eric sat back.

"That's him!" he said.

The rusty-bearded man watched Eric come, carrying his sea bag, as the taxi howled back up the road; but Eric had the feeling that the man was not sure he recognized him. He had been pounding stakes beside one of the swampy little ponds and stretching strings between them. At last Eric saw him drop his hammer and grin.

"Son of a gun!" he said.

He strode forward to seize Eric by both shoulders. His jaws were covered with a half-inch of cinnamon stubble and his skin had darkened so that his blue eyes looked faded. Eric felt joyful but foolish; every speech that came into his mind seemed either too much or too little. What he experienced chiefly was pride and relief at having finished the long quest.

"Talk about the Great Locomotive Chase!" his father chuckled. "I thought you'd gone home long ago."

Still Eric could not speak.

"A thousand miles! I can't believe it, Rick. Of course I knew you were on my trail, but I thought surely you'd given up. How did you know I hadn't gone back myself?" he asked.

"The people," Eric said. "Everywhere I went, they showed me something you'd fixed for them, and said, 'El Rojo did that.'"

Mr. Hansen laughed delightedly. "No kidding! Eric the Red, eh? Well, it's a fixit-man's paradise down here, that's for sure. I'm glad to know I was appreciated."

"Level with me," Eric said earnestly. "Did you really paddle that *panga,* or did you hitch rides on shrimp boats?"

"Well, I may have accepted a tow now and then," his father confessed, "but most of the time I was doing it the hard way—as you did, from the looks of you. Are you hungry?" he asked.

Eric massaged his middle; there was a little loose skin, not a pinch of fat. "I've been hungry ever since I traded my motorcycle to that *vagabundo* for his canoe," he sighed. "I guess hunger came with the boat."

His father laid an arm across his shoulders. "Come on up to the house. I'll scare up some lunch."

In the warm afternoon, the fields and groves of the town below them, they ate sandwiches on the long veranda. Lettuce-green, the fields of sugar cane shimmered in the sun; darker lines of mango and papaya trees swayed gracefully in the wind from the Pacific, a blue barricade in the distance.

"So now that you've caught me," Eric's father said, soberly, "what are you going to do about it?"

Eric rubbed his neck. "Funny. I had it all figured out when I left. Now I can't quite remember why I came."

"With me," said his father, "it worked just the reverse. When I left, I wasn't sure why I had to go—I just knew it was the only way out of the bag. Now that I'm here, though, I know exactly what I'm going to do."

Eric waited. They had become like a couple of *vagabundos* themselves, he thought, speaking slowly and only after sufficient thought, letting silence collect without panicking into chatter.

His father sipped some coffee. "A wise old Frenchman said that it's not what we believe about life, but how we live it. I'll go back after I've put this place on a paying basis and sold my lease. After that, I hope to spend my time doing the things I believe in—not just having opinions about them. Maybe I'll buy Pancho's agency if it's still for sale. On the other hand, maybe I won't. *Quién sabe?* But if I don't, it won't be because anybody talked me out of it."

He smiled. His teeth shone in his rusty beard. He looked younger than Eric remembered him, like the father he used to throw a ball at to get a game going.

"Did you meet the Nestors?" asked Mr. Hansen.

"Sure did. Nice people," Eric said. "After I finish summer school, I'm going to hitch-hike up to San Francisco and see Polly."

"Lovely girl," his father commented.

"I'm going to try to talk her into going to San Diego State next fall."

"Convenient," said his father. "Of course, the way things

look, you'll probably be going to City College for a while."

"Still convenient," Eric said.

For a while they ate in silence. Birds chirped in the warm afternoon, the sun burned on the canals threading the green fields below them.

"I'm going to take a shot at marine biology," Eric said, thoughtfully. "That rough-water-animal study of Dr. Nestor's kind of turns me on. 'Is tenacity innate or acquired?' That's interesting. Why does a crab or a sea anemone take all that battering, when it could move to the other side of the rock and get out of it?"

Leaning back in his chair, Eric's father nodded reflectively. "As one rough-water animal to another," he said, "I'd say that it's acquired. It comes to you somewhere between the blisters and the calluses."